PRAISE FOR YURI HERRERA

"Yuri Herrera is Mexico's greatest novelist. His spare, poetic narratives and incomparable prose read like epics compacted into a single perfect punch—they ring your bell, your being, your soul."

Francisco Goldman

"Yuri Herrera must be a thousand years old. He must have traveled to hell, and heaven, and back again. He must have once been a girl, an animal, a rock, a boy, and a woman. Nothing else explains the vastness of his understanding."

Valeria Luiselli

"My favorite of the new Mexican writers."

John Powers, NPR's *Fresh Air*

"Playful, prophetic, unnerving books that deserve to be read several times."

Eileen Battersby, *Irish Times*

"*Signs Preceding the End of the World* is short, suspenseful . . . outlandish and heartbreaking."

John Williams, *New York Times*

"Herrera's metaphors grasp the freedom, and the alarming disorientation, of transition and translation."

Maya Jaggi, *The Guardian*

"Herrera packs *The Transmigration of Bodies* with the sex, booze and nihilism of a better Simenon novella."

Sam Sacks, *Wall Street Journal*

"I was captured by *Kingdom Cons*. His writing style is like nobody else's, a unique turn of language, a kind of poetic slang . . . seeming to fall in my hands from an alternative sky."

Patti Smith

THREE NOVELS

YURI HERRERA

KINGDOM CONS

SIGNS PRECEDING THE END OF THE WORLD

THE TRANSMIGRATION OF BODIES

TRANSLATED BY LISA DILLMAN

WITH A NEW PREFACE
BY THE AUTHOR

SHEFFIELD – LONDON – NEW YORK

This special omnibus edition first published in 2021 by
And Other Stories
Sheffield – London – New York
www.andotherstories.org

Kingdom Cons: © Yuri Herrera and Editorial Periférica, 2008
First published as *Trabajos del reino* in 2008 by Editorial Periférica, Spain.
English-language translation copyright © Lisa Dillman, 2017

Signs Preceding the End of the World: © Yuri Herrera and Editorial Periférica, 2009
First published as *Señales que precederán al fin del mundo* in 2009 by Editorial Periférica, Spain.
English-language translation copyright © Lisa Dillman, 2015

The Transmigration of Bodies: © Yuri Herrera and Editorial Periférica, 2013
First published as *La transmigración de los cuerpos* in 2013 by Editorial Periférica, Spain.
English-language translation copyright © Lisa Dillman, 2016

Preface to this omnibus edition copyright © Yuri Herrera, 2021

Translation notes copyright © Lisa Dillman, 2015, 2016, 2017

"The Trick to Translating Rhythm, Tone, and Slang in *Kingdom Cons*"
first published online on *Literary Hub* on June 9, 2017.

"On the Delicate Question of Tone in *Signs Preceding the End of the World*"
first published in the first English-language edition, 2015.

"On the Genius of Yuri Herrera's Character Names in *The Transmigration of Bodies*" first published online on *Literary Hub* on July 7, 2016.

1 3 5 7 9 10 8 6 4 2

ISBN: 9781913505240

Editor of *Kingdom Cons* and *The Transmigration of Bodies*: Tara Tobler; editor of *Signs Preceding the End of the World*: Lorna Scott Fox. Typeset in Albertan Pro and Linotype Syntax by Tetragon, London. Cover Design: Tom Etherington. Printed and bound on acid-free, age-resistant Munken Premium by CPI Limited, Croydon, UK.

And Other Stories gratefully acknowledge that our work is supported using public funding by Arts Council England and that *The Transmigration of Bodies* was selected to receive financial assistance from English PEN's PEN Translates programme, supported by Arts Council England.

CONTENTS

Preface by Yuri Herrera   vii

KINGDOM CONS   1

SIGNS PRECEDING THE END OF THE WORLD   87

THE TRANSMIGRATION OF BODIES   155

Translator's Notes by Lisa Dillman   253

Parts of each of these novels were written in Pachuca, the one place I always return to, no matter where I go; the other parts were written on the Juárez–El Paso Border, in Berkeley and in New Orleans, in that order.

Every book retains some element of the place where it was written, in its breath, in its tone. But there are other places present too, within those that one invents: places where one was struck by images, moments, people who become the quantum sign, the one that art demands in order to sense the enormous truths that reside in even the most ephemeral.

The teenager, oblivious to my gaze, who I spied on for blocks, on a bus in Ciudad Juárez: he wore the proud fuzz of an incipient moustache and was sitting over the bus's middle tires, where the floor arced up over a wheel, leaning his shins on the metal hump. Resting on his knees was a staved notebook, in which he'd written notes and song lyrics. He was revising with devotion and only occasionally looked up to fix his gaze on something thousands of kilometers away. That image of a boy absorbed in his music is one that guided me as I wrote *Kingdom Cons*.

Juanita, a friend of my mother's, moved to Pachuca from El Maye, a Hñäñu community in Valle del Mezquital, in Hidalgo. She's dark, tall and strong, has huge teeth, a quick wit and a generous laugh. She had an office job that paid well for someone who lived alone, but despite being the only occupant of her home, she didn't live alone. She quit her job and went to Florida to pack chickens so she could support her community. Juanita was one of my earliest models for the tremendous women who appear in *Signs Preceding the End of the World*—migrant women, probably the most important human beings in the history of humanity.

One day in Mexico City, during the N1H1 epidemic—that Apocalypse that seems so innocuous now—I crossed Avenida de los Insurgentes with a junkman who, seeing the mask on my face, smiled derisively and began to hack dramatically. I wrote it up, just like that, in *The Transmigration of Bodies*. I hope that man, unlike the character in the book, is okay. I had nothing against him; the brief moment when we crossed paths didn't make us enemies, but it did make me see how, in an edgy city fraught with nerves, two strangers could see each other as a threat.

The novels set these places out, both the ephemeral ones and those that have names on maps, but their final shape is not theirs; the shape they ultimately take is the one that manifests mysteriously in each reader's head.

YURI HERRERA
New Orleans, Louisiana, March 2021

KINGDOM
CONS

He knew blood, and could see this man's was different. Could see it in the way he filled the space, with no urgency and an all-knowing air, as though made of finer threads. Other blood. The man took a seat at a table and his attendants fanned out in a semicircle behind him.

Lobo admired him in the waning light of day that filtered in through a small window on the wall. He had never had these people close, but was sure he'd seen this scene before. The respect this man and his companions inspired in him had been set out somewhere, the sudden sense of importance he got on finding himself so close. He recognized the way the man sat, the lofty look, the glimmer. Then he saw the jewels that graced him and knew: he was a King.

The one time Lobo had gone to the pictures he saw a movie with a man like this: strong, sumptuous, dominating the things of the world. He was a King, and around him everything became meaningful. Men gave their lives for him, women gave birth for him; he protected and bestowed, and in the kingdom, through his grace, each and every subject had a precise place. But those accompanying this King were more than vassals. This was his Court.

Lobo felt envy, the bad kind first and the good kind after, because suddenly he saw that this was the most important day of his life. Never before had he been near one of those who gave life meaning, made it all tally up. Never even had the hope. Ever since his parents had brought him here from who knows where and then abandoned him to his fate, life had been a counting off of days of dust and sun.

A voice thick with phlegm distracted his gaze from the King: a drunk, ordering him to sing. Lobo complied, effortlessly at first, still trembling with excitement; but soon, from the same, he sang like never before, pulling words out from inside as though pronouncing them for the first time, as though overcome by the ecstasy of having happened upon them. He felt the King's eyes on his back and the cantina fall silent; people put their dominoes facedown on tables to listen. He sang a song and the drunk demanded Another and then Another and Another and Another, and with each one Lobo sang more inspired, and the drunk got more drunk. At times he joined in, at times he spat into the sawdust and laughed with the old soak there with him. Finally he said Okay, and Lobo held out his hand. The drunk paid and Lobo saw it was short and held out his hand once more.

"That's it, songbird. What I got left is for one more shot. Just thank your saints you got that much."

Lobo was used to it. These things happened. And he was about to turn away in What Can You Do resignation, when he heard from behind:

"Pay the artist."

Lobo turned to see the King holding the drunk in his gaze. He said it calm. It was a simple order, but the man didn't know enough to stop.

"What artist?" he said. "Only thing I see here is this fool and I already paid him."

"Don't get smart, friend," the King's voice hardened. "Pay him and shut it."

The drunk got up and staggered to the King's table. His men went on alert, but the King sat unflustered. The drunk struggled to focus and then said:

"I know you. I heard what they say."

"That a fact? And what do they say?"

The drunk laughed. Clumsily scratched a cheek.

"Nah. Not your business I'm talking about, everybody knows that . . . Talking about the other."

And he laughed once more.

The King's face clouded. He tilted his head back, got up. Signaled his entourage to stay put. Approached the drunk and grabbed his chin. The man tried to twist free: no luck. The King put his lips to the drunk's ear and said:

"Actually, I don't think you heard a thing. You know why? Because dead men have very poor hearing."

The King put his gun to him as tho feeling the man's gut, and fired. A simple shot. Nonchalant. The drunk opened his eyes wide, tried to steady himself on a table, slipped and fell. The King turned to the boozer with him.

"You got something to say too?"

The man snatched his hat and fled, hands high in a Didn't See A Thing. The King bent over the corpse, rifled through a pocket, pulled out a wad of bills. He peeled off a few, handed them to Lobo, replaced the rest.

"Artist, take your due," he said.

Lobo took the bills without looking down. He was staring

at the King, drinking him in. And kept watching as the King signaled his crew and they filed slowly out of the cantina. Lobo gazed at the swinging doors. And thought that from now on there was a new reason why calendars were senseless: no date meant a thing besides this one. Because finally he'd found his place in the world. And because he'd heard something about a secret, which he damn well wanted to keep.

Dust and sun. Silence. A sorry house where no one exchanged words. His parents a couple of strays who got lost in the same corner, nothing to say to each other. That was why the words started to pile up, first in Lobo's mouth and then in his hands. For him school was brief, a place where he sensed the harmony of letters, the rhythms that strung them together and split them apart. It was a private discovery, since he couldn't see the lines on the chalkboard clearly and the teacher took him for a fool, and he confined himself to the solitude of his notebook. And it was out of sheer passion that he mastered the ways of syllables and accents, before being ordered to earn his keep on the street, offering rhymes in exchange for pity, for coins.

The street was hostile territory, a muffled struggle whose rules made no sense; he managed to endure it by repeating sweet refrains in his head and inhabiting the world through its public words: posters, papers sold on street corners, signs. These were his antidote to chaos. He'd stop on the sidewalk and run his eyes again and again over any random string of words to forget the fierce environs around him.

One day his father put the accordion in his hands. Coldly, as tho instructing him on how to unjam a door, he taught Lobo to combine the chord buttons on the left with the basses on the right, how the bellows trap and release air to shape the sounds.

"Now hold it good," he said, "This is your bread."

The next day his father went to the other side. They waited in vain. Then his mother crossed without so much as a promise of return. They left him the accordion so he could make his way in the cantinas, and it was there he learned that while boleros can get by with a sweet face, corridos require bravado and acting out the story as you sing. He also learned the following truths: Life is a matter of time and hardship. There is a God who says Deal with it, cause this is the way it is. And perhaps the most important: Steer clear of a man about to vomit.

He never took notice of the calendar. It seemed absurd because days were all alike: do the rounds of the tables, offer songs, hold out your hand, fill your pockets with change. Dates earned a name only when someone took pity on themselves or another by pulling out steel and shortening the wait. Or when Lobo discovered hairs cropping up or things getting bigger on his body at will. Or when pain hacksawed his skull and struck him down for hours at a time. Endings and eccentricities were the most notable way to order time. That was how he spent it.

That, and learning blood. He could detect its curdle in the parasites who said, Come, come little boy, and invited him into the corner; the way it congealed in the veins of fraidycats who smiled for no reason; the way it turned to water in the bodies of those who played the same heartache on the jukebox, over and over again; the way it dried out like a stone in lowlifes just aching to throw down.

Every night Lobo went back to the place where he boxed down, to stare at the cardboard and feel his words grow.

He started writing songs about stuff that happened to others. He knew nothing of love but he'd heard stories, so he'd mention it amid wisdom and proverbs, give it a beat, and sell it. But it was all imitation, a mirror held up to lives overheard. And tho he suspected there was more he could do with his songs, he didn't know how to go deeper. It had all been said before. Why bother. All he could do was wait, carry on and wait. For what? A miracle.

It was exactly as he'd always envisioned palaces to be. Supported by columns, paintings and statues in every room, animal skins draped over sofas, gold doorknockers, a ceiling too high to touch. And more than that, it was people. So many people, striding down corridors. This way and that, attending to affairs or looking to shine. People from far and wide, from every corner of the earth, people from beyond the desert. Word of God there were even some who had seen the sea. And women who walked like leopards, and giant warriors, their faces decorated with scars; there were Indians and blacks; he actually saw a dwarf. Lobo sidled up to circles, he pricked up his ears, thirsting to learn. He heard tell of mountains, of jungles, of gulfs, of summits, in singsong accents entirely new to him: yesses like shesses, words with no esses, some whose tone soared up so high and sank so low it seemed each sentence was a journey: it was clear they were from nowhere near here.

He'd been out this way long ago, when still with his parents. But back then it was a dump, a hellhole of waste and infection. No way to know it would become a beacon. The royalty of a king determined these things: the man had settled among simple folk and turned the filth to splendor. Approached from afar, the Palace exploded from the edge of the desert in a vast pageantry of gardens, gates and walls. A gleaming city on the fringes of a city in squalor, a city that seemed to reproduce its misfortune on street after street. Here, the people who came and went thrust their shoulders back with the air of those who know that theirs is a prosperous dominion.

The Artist had to find a way to stay.

He'd learned there was to be a party that night, set off for the Palace, and played his only card.

"I come to sing for the chief."

The guards glanced at him like a stray dog. Didn't even open their mouths. But the Artist recognized one from the cantina encounter and could tell that the man recognized him, too.

"You saw he liked my songs. Let me sing for him and it'll be good for you, watch."

The guard wrinkled his brow a few seconds, as if imagining his fortune. Then he approached the Artist, shoved him to the wall and frisked. Satisfied that he was harmless, the guard said:

"He better like you." Then dragged him in, and when the Artist was on his way, he warned, "Round here, you blow it, you're fucked."

Finding no good space for himself at the party he thought it better to wander among the guests. Until the music started and a sea of sombreros rose up, looking for action on the dance floor. Couples configured and the Artist found himself ricocheted from hips and elbows. Some fiesta, he thought. He'd scoot to one side and a couple would come at him in three quick steps, scoot to the other and the next one tripped him on a turn. Finally he managed to corner himself and take

11

it in without getting in the way: so elegant, the sombreros; so suave, the violence with which those thighs pressed together; and so much gold, dripping off the guests.

Awestruck, the question took him by surprise.

"Like what you see, amigo?"

The Artist turned and saw a blondish man, weathered and elegant, who sat in his chair giving him a What Do You Think? face. He nodded. The man pointed to an empty seat beside him and outstretched his hand.

He said his name and then stressed:

"Jeweler. All the gold you see, I made. You?"

"I make songs," the Artist replied. And no sooner was this out of his mouth than he sensed that he, too, could begin repeating, after his name: Artist, I make songs.

"Have a drink, amigo; plenty here to get you going."

Yes, indeed, it was a banquet. On every table was whiskey, rum, brandy, tequila, beer, and plenty of sotol; no one could complain about the hospitality. Girls in black miniskirts topped glasses the moment they were raised, or if you wanted you could go over to a table and pour as much as you liked. The promise of carne asada and roast kid hung in the air as well. A waitress put a beer in his hand, but he didn't so much as touch it.

"Now don't go thinking they paint it red here all the time," said the Jeweler. "The King prefers kicking it with the people, in old saloons, but today's a special day."

He glanced side to side before leaning conspiratorially toward the Artist, tho everybody knew:

"Two kingpins coming in to make a deal and he's got to treat them right, go all out."

The Jeweler leaned back in his chair, smug, and the Artist once more nodded and looked around. He felt no envy for the gold-worked belt buckles and snakeskin boots the guests had on, tho they were dazzling; but the outfits the musicians on stage wore, those were something else: black and white spur-print shirts with leather fringe. There by the band, close enough to make requests, he spotted the King, majesty chiseled into his stone cheekbones. He was laughing raucously with the two Lords flanking him, both of whom might have given the impression of power, but no, not the force or commanding air of the King. There was one more man at their table, one who'd also been there at the cantina the other day. Less elegant than the Lords, or more round-the-way: no sombrero, no buckle.

"That's the Top Dog," said the Jeweler, seeing where he was looking. "The King's right-hand man. Punk's got balls, fearless as they come, but he's cocky as shit."

Better be, if he's the Heir, the Artist thought.

"But don't say I said so, amigo," the Jeweler went on, "no gossip allowed. Way it works here is, you make nice with the pack, you'll do fine. Like you and me right now, we just made friends, right?"

Something in the Jeweler's tone put the Artist on edge, and now he did not nod. The Jeweler seemed to sense this and changed the subject. Told him he made jewelry only to order, whatever his clients wanted, and that's what you should do, too, Artist, make everyone look good. The Artist was about to respond when the guard who'd let him in approached.

"It's time," he said. "Hustle up, and ask the boys to accompany you."

13

The Artist stood nervously and walked to the stage. On the way he sensed the shape and the scent of a different sort of woman but refused to turn his head and look, tho the heat lingered. He stood among the musicians, said Just follow my lead, and launched in. People already knew the story, but no one had ever sung it. He'd asked endless questions to find out what went down, to compose this song and present it to the King. It told of his mettle and his heart, put to the test in a hail of bullets, and had a happy ending not only for the King but also for the down-and-outs he kept under his wing. Beneath that enormous vaulted ceiling his voice projected, taking on depths it never had in the cantinas. He sung his song with the faith of a hymn, the certainty of a sermon, and above all he made sure it was catchy, so people would learn it with their feet and their hips, and so they, too, would sing it later.

When he was done, the crowd showered him with whistles and applause, the elegant musicians clapped him on the back and the Lords accompanying the King headbobbed in contentment and pooched their lips in—the Artist hoped—envy. He climbed down to pay his respects. The King looked him in the eye and the Artist bowed his head.

"I knew you had talent as soon as I saw you," said the King, who, it was known, never forgot a face. "All your songs that good, Artist?"

"I do my best, sir," the Artist stammered.

"Well, don't hold back, then: write; stick with the good guys and it'll all go your way." He nodded to another man standing nearby and said, "Take care of him."

The Artist bowed again and followed the man, fit to burst into tears and blinded by bright lights and his future. Then he took a deep breath, said to himself, It's really happening, and came back down to earth. That was when he remembered the silhouette that had caught his attention. He looked around. And at the same time, the man spoke.

"I'm the Manager. Take care of accounts. You never ask Señor for money, you ask me. Tomorrow I'll take you to a man who does the recording. You give him everything you write," the Manager stopped, seeing the Artist's eyes wander. "And don't stick your snout where it doesn't belong; don't even look at a woman who doesn't belong to you."

"Who does that one belong to?" The Artist pointed to a trussed-up girl to cover his tracks.

"That one," said the Manager like he was distracted, like his mind was on something else, "belongs to whoever needs her."

He turned back to the Artist, measuring him up, then called the girl over and said, "The Artist here has made Señor very happy; treat him well."

And falling prey to an absurd panic, fearful of what he sensed was about to happen, but more fearful of succumbing to that other aroma, the Artist accepted the Girl's delicate hand and allowed himself to be led from the hall.

What was all that about having been here before, in another life? About God having a chosen path for each of us, since the start of time? For a while, the idea kept the Artist up nights, until he beheld an image in the Palace that freed him: an exquisite apparatus, a turntable with diamond stylus that played thirtythrees and belonged to the Jeweler, who one weekend forgot to turn it off, and, when he noticed two days later, found it no longer worked.

That's it, thought the Artist. That's all we are. Contraptions that get forgotten, serve no purpose. Maybe God put the needle on the record and then went off to nurse a hangover. The Artist already had clear that there was no one high in the sky or down underground looking out for him, that it was each to their own, but now, at the Court, he was starting to see that you could have a little fun before the diamond turned to dust. Not just wait around.

The gift the King had given him days earlier was the sign: his wait was over.

The Girl's blood was a delicate brook trickling over pebbles, but her body inclined to an uncommon skill that took the Artist's breath away for two days straight. You're learning, she'd say, and after each swoon he'd want to drop dead or get married, and would weep. The girl portended so much world, even in the farflung way she spoke, and she'd laugh: I just gave you a nudge and out came a stud, songman. She, too, had been saved by the King; rescued from a hovel by the bridge and brought to the Palace. Now the Girl named her enthusiasm with words newly learned:

"It's amped here, singer, it's trick as shit; man, it's all sauce; it's wicked, slick, I mean this place is *tight*; people here come from everywhere and everybody's down."

How she thirsted for happiness, but the Artist could see in her eyes that she also yearned for other affections, for things not found in the Palace.

For the first few days almost all the Artist did was eat. From the start, he would show up in the dining room when the guards were being fed and share their rations. But all that did was awaken a hunger that had long since skulked within. The Girl told him to do as she had, when she first arrived with a stomach empty for years: turn up as soon as the King, who also ate there—occasionally even with the others—was done, and finish anything he'd left untouched. There were always several dishes, and the chef allowed them to be eaten provided nothing was taken out of the hall.

Spending so much time there, the Artist began to hear the stories people told as they lingered over the table after mealtime, and he used them to weave the fabric of his songs.

"Fools take me for a chump, I lose my shit," one said. "The other week a mule tried to short me, so I took a pair of pliers and tore off his thumbs. No need to kill him, but at least now he'll have a hard time counting his cash. Shitbag deserved it for playing dirty, right?"

"Deep down, I'm a sentimental guy," said another. "So to keep track of the dogs I smoke, I pull a tooth from each one and stick it in my dashboard; wonder how many smiles I'll end up with in my truck."

They loved each other like brothers, they scratched each other's bellies, they gave each other nicknames. One was a guard who'd been caught poking a calf so they called him the Saint, since animals loved him.

"Damn, Saint, you're sick," they taunted, "I just realized this barbecue tastes like you."

Some poor fatty who'd had his arms ripped off as payback now worked there as a messenger; he wore a backpack and roamed the Palace making deliveries. They called him Danger Boy and when the guards saw him coming they'd shout, "Danger! Danger!" And Danger Boy would laugh.

The Artist realized that people saw him only when he sang or they wanted someone to hear how tough they were; and that was good, because it meant he could see how things worked in the Court. Like a cat in a new house, he gradually began to venture out beyond the dining hall and the Girl's room. He got lost constantly. The Palace was a simple grid with a courtyard at the center but there were so many unpredictable corridors that sometimes when he thought he was headed one way, he'd end up at the other end of the building. To keep from being overwhelmed by the Palace's grandiosity, the Artist began carrying one of the Girl's tiny mirrors, observing details over his shoulder: carved furniture, metal doors, candelabras. That was also how he was able to observe, unnoticed, visitors from the cities, suits with briefcases, officers of the law who'd come for their kickback, the business never ended. It was like being invisible.

He discovered that in addition to the King, his guards, the girls and the servants, several courtiers lived there as well. The one he always bumped into was the Manager, ever busy ensuring things ran smoothly. He took him to meet a band that was to record his lyrics so he could make sure the songs came out the way he'd heard them in his head; he even recorded a song himself.

"Then the Journalist will promote your music with his contacts on the radio," the Manager said.

The Artist went back to his digs only once, to keep the dogs from taking over his box; but since no one seemed to notice him at the Palace, or else they'd grown used to him, he brought his few belongings—a notebook with his songs, a dressy vest—and settled in.

To no courtier did he deny his talents. He wrote a corrido for the house Gringo, a master at devising routes for product. The Gringo had cozied up to a gang of young buzz-seekers who crossed over every Friday to kick it this side of the wall. You got a caretaker in me, you sure do; they trusted. The wildest one was a freckled kid, son of a Consul who the Gringo would send back home with fatherly affection and car seats stuffed with weed. Nice little setup, till freckles got lost in a fleapit shooting gallery. Top-notch corrido. He wrote one for the Doctor, the Court's Número Uno stitch-it man, who the King sent to treat a triggerman that got shotgunned in the stomach. The punk was double-crossing, but didn't know they knew. The Doctor eased his pain but also slipped in a gift for the shits he worked for. So when the two-timer went to see his handlers, the poison in his belly blew up on cue and brought them all down, no glory. He wrote one for Pocho, the guy with gringo airs who used to say, as if it were his name: I didn't cross the border; the border crossed me. Pocho had been a cop on the other side but one day he found himself in a jam, and justice shone its light on him: three of his men had surrounded the King, who was prepared to die with honor rather than go down, but a snitch came up to Pocho and said, Who says you got to be on their side? So he emptied his clip into the uniformed thugs, and has been with the good guys ever since.

To no courtier did he deny his talents, but the Artist recounted the feats of each man without forgetting who made it all possible. Sure, you're down, because the King allows it. Sure, you're brave, because the King inspires you. The only time he didn't mention the King's name was when he wrote little love songs that some courtier requested in hushed tones. After, they'd slap him on the back or hook his neck and say, Whatever you want, Artist. Of course he also couldn't use the King's name when he wrote words for little jobs requiring letters. Things like We're sending our cop, so don't sweat the authorities—and he knew to spell authorities au; or Write your personal details here, on a bogus passport. The Artist knew how to make himself useful. And knew how to gain respect: if he said Not just now, I'm working on a corrido, the courtiers listened.

Only two men in the Court didn't ask for corridos. And damn if they didn't deserve them. He saw them together on a Palace balcony tossing back a couple of whiskeys. When he told the Heir he had a story almost ready for him, the man said:

"Later." Clenched his jaw as if holding back the words that followed and simply repeated, "Later."

He was spine-chilling, the Heir, with his impeccable solid-colored shirts, never a single stain, tho his eyes foretold explosion. The man contained himself as if always on his best behavior.

And the other one who declined, the Journalist, the man who maintained the King's good name, said:

"Better not, because if you paint my picture then I'm no use. Imagine: if people on the outside find out I'm on the inside, who's going to believe I don't know what's what?"

The Artist understood. He had to let the man do his job. In order to keep fools entertained with clean lies, the Journalist had to make them seem true. But the real news was the Artist's job, the stuff of corridos, and there were so many yet to sing that he could forget whatever didn't serve the King.

"No offense," the Journalist said, "I don't mean to insult you. And since you like to write so much, I'm going to bring you some books, if I may."

The Artist could feel his guts seize up in excitement, but he was good at concealing things so you couldn't tell.

"You'll love them, just wait," said that Journalist. "When a person likes words, they're like booze for your ears."

Just then all three turned their heads, because down the hall came the King, at a furious pace, looking haggard. He was followed by a woman with long gray hair and a long dress; badass, with a blistering air. The King stopped for a second, turned to look as tho surprised to see them there, then continued on his way and entered the room at the end of the hall. It's time, the woman said, and then followed him. They slammed the door.

The Artist hadn't seen him since the day of the dance. He hadn't missed the King's presence because the King was always present: in the devotion with which he was mentioned; in his orders, which were all carried out; in the luster of the place.

"There they go," said the Journalist, pulling on his drink. "This about the Traitor or is it the same old thing?"

The Heir gripped his glass and nodded but seemed to be responding to nothing.

"That witch," he finally mumbled. And then, when it seemed he wasn't going to add anything else: "But things are changing."

The Artist, who knew to keep his mouth shut, gazed out at the desert and didn't move until he knew that the others had gone back into the Palace. Then with feline patience, he stared at the door the King and the Witch had disappeared behind. Not a sound. He approached, trying to see shadows in the light streaming under the door, pressed his ear. Nothing. He *knew* he shouldn't go in, but his urge beat out his fear and, heart pounding, he went to open the door, stopping his hand just before it touched the handle and jerking it back as tho he'd been burned.

He went to find the Girl. On the way to her room he caught whiff of the same scent as the other night, and on turning a corner the aroma came to life for a few seconds: first it hit him like a gust of insolence, eyes that devoured him then spat him out; then it was harmony, long hair pulled back and a spine that curved in the start of a curl; and then a sudden frost that numbed his gut. He kept walking, instinctively, without thinking, floating, and when he got to the Girl asked mechanically about the intrigue, though he'd already forgotten it. She said:

"They say there's some hotshit who didn't like the new deal, I don't know; I heard he's selling in the plaza without the King's permission. Can you believe that? Idiotic, disturbing the peace like that . . . What's wrong?"

The Artist took a deep breath and this time asked the question that was really on his mind:

"Who is she?"

No clarification required. The Girl sat in fuming silence for a few seconds and then said:

"Some commoner. A tramp."

words as a visual object

They are. There. So many letters together. His. Put there for no reason but to penetrate his brain. They are. There. Milling the sheets between rolls of insomnia, they signal, scratching at the wasted white of the paper, at his eyes. And what was each sheet if not a working tool, like a saw for someone who builds tables, a gat for someone who takes lives? Ah, but never this bluff of sand, the spirit and ambition to uncover. So many letters there. They are. There they are. They are a glimmer. How they jostle together and overflow, soaking each other and enveloping his eyes in an uproar of reasons. No matter if they're perfect, or unruly, they incriminate, fearing disarray: words. So many words. His. An uproar of signs bound together. They are a constant light. There. They are. (Books were something he already knew about, but they had spurned him, like an unwelcoming country. And now he'd let himself be led by the hand to the council of secrets. A constant light.) Each with its own radiance, each speaking the true name in its own way. Even the most false, even the most fickle. Aha. No. Not just there to penetrate his brain. There. They are a constant light. The way to other boxes, far away. The road to ears hidden right here. (Like the bugs that bite him.) No. Not just there to amuse his eyes or entertain his ear. They are a constant light. They are the lighthouse flare cast over stones

25

at his command, they are a lantern that searches, then stops, and caresses the earth, and they show him the way to make the most of the service that is his to render.

poems AS ghosts
poems AS Healing objects
poems AS historical markers

It was like an omen: the day they skewered Pocho's head the pain that had wracked the Artist's own since he was a kid came back full force. Hit him like a two-by-four, knocked him out. Even the cricket chirps were deafening and no witches' brew could ease the pain. At the Girl's alarm the Doctor came, inspected the Artist's pupils in search of diagnosis. Leave me, Doc, leave me, it'll pass, said the Artist; and the Doctor asked When did it start and how often and brought on by what, and prescribed pills to soothe him and said:

"You need tests, I'll talk to the Manager so he can fix it up with the hospital, meanwhile, take the medicine."

Screw the medicine, no way was the Artist going to take it, not him. He wouldn't even drink tepid water. He knew: Deal with it, this is just the way it is. Let others find elixirs for their sorrows or pains, he was no judge; but he chose to govern his insides on his own. He'd already had his go at tinctures: smack from some well-off drunks, the kind who are fast friends after a bottle and three songs. The Artist had lost all sense of distance, and music—his music—sounded like moaning. It scared him so bad not to know his own body that he resolved: no venom, no matter what. He handpatted at the Doctor to say Sure, sure, so that the man would leave him alone, and fell asleep.

Hours later he awoke with the terrifying clarity that told him, from the second he heard the first screams: something awful was going down.

He followed the frantic mob to the Palace gates. And before he saw Pocho's body, the Artist sensed the crowd's fear. Very few voices broke the courtiers' petrified silence, swearing as they stood beside the body. His eyes were open and his arms crossed as though he were cold. A curved dagger went in one ear and out the other, with almost no blood. There was no bag or blanket, as usual, and they hadn't tied his hands, nor could you see any singemarks from the wires used to make men talk. Behind the throng came the King with his retinue. The Heir shouted, loud, and the sea of rubberneckers parted. The King observed Pocho. He stood there awhile, hands on his waist, with the expression of a man who wished he hadn't already seen it all. Then he said:

"Take him in." And strode back to the Palace.

The Heir stayed back to ask: Who was on guard, What was the truck like, How many were there, And you, what did you do. Not a soul had seen a thing. He ordered two of the guards to be taken in to make sure they didn't know more than they said and then left. Cold. Too calm for all that rage, thought the Artist. But I bet he knows what he's doing. He, too, followed the entourage to the Palace chapel, where the Doctor was extracting the dagger from Pocho and saying: Never seen anything like it. Then the Father arrived. The Artist hadn't met him yet, tho he knew of the services he lent the Court in exchange for the King's money, funding churches to get the poor hooked on heaven. Those in hats took them off and made the sign of the cross. The Father blessed Pocho quietly and then said, louder:

"What path is this we're on?"

The courtiers said Amen tho it was out of place, and then the King entered. Without waiting for the order almost everyone filed out, and just the Witch, the Father, the Heir and the Gringo remained in the room. The Artist stood back in the shadows and kept quiet.

"This was those bastards from the south," said the Gringo. The Traitor could never have pulled this off alone; they have to be backing him."

"If they want war, give it to them," said the Witch, who was the only one not looking at the corpse but at the King's eyes, her gaze a tense rope.

The King bent over and brushed his fingers through Pocho's hair, said something to him without speaking, just moving his lips. Suddenly he turned to the Heir. How do you read this?

"We can take down whoever we need to," he said, "but what if that's what they're looking for? Whose interests are served by a war? Not ours, I tell you that."

"Coward!" spat the Witch. "They bring a body to your door and you don't retaliate? Those traitors challenge your Lord and you do nothing?"

The Heir cut her off. "That's not the way we kill," pointing to Pocho's wound, "which means that's not the way they kill. You ask me, this is about something else."

"Listen," the King stepped in, addressing the Gringo, "you're going to find out what else Pocho was into on the other side. We've got to make sure we get it right, don't want to find out this was payback for some shit from back in the day. Meanwhile, find me the Traitor, he's in for it anyway, but don't bring him down till I say so."

"If we wait . . . " the Witch protested, but the King interrupted her.

"I said we wait. You don't know war."

Like saying shut up. The King took the Father by one
shoulder and said:

"Bury him for me, the Manager will give you what you
need for the box."

"And what I still need for my ranchito . . . " the Father
slipped in. The King nodded, turned and left the chapel. The
others followed, with the exception of the Father. The Artist
emerged from the shadows and stood beside him.

"Probably deserved it," said the Father to Pocho's remains.

The words made the Artist flinch, like a slap. He left the
chapel without a word, hoping that it would be taken as an
affront but knowing that it wouldn't, since he was invisible;
but the Father's lack of judgment offended him. If he knew
one thing it was that in the course of life, sooner or later,
you cause pain, and it was better to decide up front who you
cause it to, like the King. Who was brave enough to accept
it? Who bore the cross for the rest? He was their mantle, the
wound that took the pain that others may not hurt. They
couldn't fool the Artist: he had grown up suffering at the
hands of badge and uniform, had endured the humiliation
of the well-to-do—until the King came along. So what if the
man moved poison when they asked for it on the other side?
Let them have it. Let them take it. What had they ever done
for the good guys?

"Probably deserved it," the Artist hissed in rage, and then
thought: if there's one thing we deserve, it's a heaven that's
real.

The boss was coming back, the one they'd done a deal with, and to keep spirits up, the King arranged amusements. No only were the guests supplied with hooch, smack and women, but they set up a casino and organized a shooting contest.

The whole Court moved to the grounds. They brought cages with dozens and dozens of doves, black ones that wouldn't get lost in the desert glare. The King, the Heir and the other boss and his top dog positioned themselves, shotguns aimed up at the sky. Each marksman had a guard in charge of fetching the pieces he shot and putting them in a sack behind him. The cages were opened and suddenly there came a great skyward flutter and a hail of bullets. The crowd clapped each time the shooters hit a bird and it fell, leaving a dark trail.

The boss was a good shot, even allowed himself the luxury of taunting his birdboy, firing at his feet while shouting:

"Ándele, ándele, ándele, bastard, time to earn your keep."

The spectators whooped at his antics, while the boss—laughing his head off, hardly taking aim and not stopping to see if he'd hit—fired his gun nonstop, up and down, sky and ground. The fetchers to'd and fro'd with the pieces, sometimes squabbling, ripping a bird. Even then it was clear that the King, tho he took careful aim and almost always hit his mark, was not fast enough, and he was losing.

A sequence of images flew through the Artist's brain in quick succession: the King defeated, the scorn and petulance of the no-account winner, the faces of the Courtiers—dejected, when yet again it rained on their parade. More than a reflex, his reaction was an instantaneous understanding of how he could be of service. He scooted out in front of the spectators and, while everyone was gazing at the hullabaloo up above, edged over to the King's sack while his fetcher was out in the field. The Artist crouched and pulled a bird from the bag and then stood there, waiting, until the King turned and, utterly astonished, saw what he was doing. Then the Artist sidestepped repeatedly, his back still to the crowd, until he was at the capo's sack. Now he waited for the capo to see him and then swiftly, wearing a guilty face, chucked that same bird into his sack. There was one more cage to go, but the boss was no longer laughing; instead he'd turned to stare at each sack between shots. When there were no more doves in the sky, the kingpin approached the King.

"What the—?" he asked, face uncomprehending.

The King lifted his chin a bit: what are you on about? The boss then demanded:

"Show me your hands."

The Artist held them out, bloody, and the King wiped off his innocent expression, burst out laughing as though he'd just gotten the joke, and clapped the capo on the back.

"Don't be angry, friend, it's just that my boy here told me you'd been given a faulty shotgun by mistake." The King opened his arms wide and added, "And that's not how we roll here. At my house the guest always wins."

The capo stood in suspense, as if waiting for a conclusion to draw itself. Then his laughter grew louder and louder, and he embraced the King.

"Sly fox! They told me you were a gentleman." And he turned to the public and pointed to the King: "This is your winner! This is your winner right here!"

The public applauded without having heard what the bosses had said, happy because they seemed happy. The King beamed in his blue shirt with bright reds and yellows. He invited the boss to a game of poker and the crowd trailed after to the casino. But halfway there he stopped and turned, hands on hips, gazing intently at the Artist, his face one of surprise and satisfaction.

"So you're a crafty bastard," he whispered, and turned back to the Palace.

"So, does a girl have to carry a gun for you to write her a song?" said she, the Commoner.

Staring at him. She was staring right at him, and the Artist didn't know how to handle the astonishment he felt with her almond eyes trained his way. He stood frozen until she arched her eyebrows like this—Well . . . ?—as though aiming a cannon at his chest, and then he replied.

"It's not about the guns, it's the stories. What's yours?"

"I don't tell the truth to anyone in this place," she said, and started walking back down the hall that the Artist had ended up on. The Artist followed a little ways, finding and discarding the precise words he needed to prolong their conversation. They went out to the grounds, strolled by a fountain in whose center stood a god spitting water through its mouth, carried on to a maze of shrubs that spelled out the King's name, and on reaching a swimming pool tiled in mosaic made to look like leaves and grass, the Artist got it right.

"So don't tell the truth, tell me lies."

The Commoner turned and stared for a second, astonished. She leaned over the water as if searching for someone to take it out on. Then she gazed out at the perimeter, the electrified fence, the desert; and after awhile she said:

"What's the point? You might end up believing me."

They walked to where the King's collection was. There were snakes, tigers, crocodiles, an ostrich and, in a bigger cage, almost its own garden, a peacock.

"His favorite," said the Commoner, swooping out an open hand, ironic. The animal flapped its wings and the Artist saw that it had a small bandage around its foot. He was about to ask how the animal got wounded there and who took the time to treat it, but the Commoner said:

"I need to go see my mother." Seeing the question in his eyes she added, "The one who's always with him."

The Artist shivered a bit at the hatred with which she'd referred to the witch, and more at the confirmation that they were blood. He opted not to follow her when she returned to the Palace as if she'd been out alone. Still, tho she'd turned her back to him, she had left a trail of pebbles with which to find her: rage and secrets; she'd looked at him.

The days that followed would have been the happiest in the Artist's life since his encounter with the King were it not for the fact that they were also the most unsettled. Suddenly his lyric urge abandoned him and his ear served only to listen for the Commoner's footsteps, his eyes only to surveil corners, his hands only to tremble at her absence. But he pretended. He aped the self that kept its cool.

When he came across the Commoner he stuck to her side and they spoke on the go: she wore loose men's pants and uncinched shirts, hiding her body, but when she moved the cloth and her skin met and the Artist could see it. They almost never sat, and when they did the Commoner would sink into her chair as if impressing her shape.

That was the way they roamed the Palace. Treacherously,

the Artist slowly learned her curves as they ran through topics and rooms. In the ballroom he grazed her forearm and told her of his parents on the other side of the line; in the game room he brushed her back with an elbow as she spoke of when she'd had friends, as a girl; in the armory he stroked her hair and told her stories of cantinas—but the topic made her stop listening, for some reason she switched off and slowly began to close her eyes, curling up like a kitten, and the Artist felt the urge to accompany her silence, for in it he understood her a little better; when they spoke of the Witch his thigh glanced her thigh as they rambled around the boardroom with built-in cantina, the study with built-in cantina, the balcony with built-in cantina, the dining room with built-in cantina, and the cantina proper, so magnificent.

"She frees him of a demon," said the Commoner. And she told him how, long ago, when he was not yet who he would become, the King had asked her mother for help and the two of them had left her father, a good man who was therefore a useless man, and now a lonely man.

From that moment on, the soundtrack of his desire took on a strident tone, because he realized he had no permission to touch the Commoner: the King had not consented, and without his say-so things could never move forward. He had gotten close to the Commoner because he took the Girl at her word when she'd said that that was what she was: one of many. And now what was he doing? Not only longing to touch her but to be with her, to share her solitude. He stood at a distance when they strolled but could not calm his trembling. She knew it when he stared at her perfect little nose, aching to trace a finger across her eyebrows.

"If there's a fly on my face, get it off," the Commoner said, and the Artist hid his hands like a thief. She laughed tenderly, perhaps, and then led him to a room lined with empty shelves.

"The library," she stated with absolutely no emphasis, as tho she hadn't said anything at all. Yes, there were a few sheets of paper, a bible, maps, newspapers with stories of dead men, a magazine with a color photo of the members of the Court at a wedding. Mentally, the Artist unfolded a scrap of paper on which he scribbled the idea for a song about the King and his men planning war.

Soon the Artist began sweating distress, because he could feel the Commoner's body getting closer: as they gamboled by the Girl's room, which at the time was still his, too, she sunk her nails lightly into his waist; passing the guards' barracks she pressed her face to his at the slightest pretext; in the trucks' loading bay he endured the tips of her breasts pointing against his back. That very afternoon he decided to take off the brakes, to find her and come undone in confessions. He caught sight of her on the same balcony where he'd heard the Heir and the Journalist scheming, set off so she couldn't get away, and a few meters before he reached the corner where there was nothing but the balcony and the locked room, felt someone jerk his shoulder.

"I was looking for you," the Journalist said. "There's a problem with your songs."

The Artist turned to fling off the hand that restrained him, looked at the spot where he should have found the Commoner, and a second before he could confirm it, knew that he wouldn't find her, knew that there, people disappeared.

They didn't want his songs. Jockeys at the station said his words were coarse, his good guys were bad. Or they said yes, but no: they liked the lyrics but had orders to shut his groove down. It wasn't the Artist's unbuttery voice, he'd only recorded one little tune; other singers, finer voices, were tasked with giving his songs a smoother sound. One of the DJs said to the Journalist, hey, between you and me, the Supreme G is turning the screws tight these days: a show for the gringos, temporary hush-hush till the advertisers cool down. Couldn't he ask the Artist to clean it up a little, write sweeter songs, less crude?

"Don't look at me," said the Journalist, "I'm just letting you know, and now I'm taking you to Señor so we can figure out what to do about this . . . He'll be free in a minute."

So they didn't want him, thought the Artist, so he was chump change for the big-money men, so he made their ears itch. He'd been insulted a hundred times before, only this time he wasn't humiliated: he swaggered, felt superior. He clenched his jaw and suddenly could see it all clearly. It was the rejection of others that defined him. Shit, so what if his singing pained them, in the end what the Artist enjoyed was gazing into the eyes of his audience, bringing their bones to life on the dance floor, singing to the people, real people.

His footsteps and those of the Journalist rang out on the marble: an energetic echo. The Artist spouted off under his breath and as the marble sped by underfoot he got madder and madder, and surer of himself, as if the answer lay waiting at the end of the hall. In the Gallery.

"Here we are," said the Journalist.

People lined up, coming in through a big door, in shawls and tattered trousers, carrying kids, their faces blank but shining slightly with faith. The Gallery was a controlled chaos, alarmed yet deferential, and smelled of dirt and salt, and a kind of curdled heat.

"Where were you?" demanded the Jeweler the second he saw him walk in. "Don't you know what today is?"

The Artist didn't know, and felt ashamed since he saw that somehow it was his duty to know, for as soon as he entered and sensed the atmosphere, he got goosebumps and suspected that he was not alone in his anger, that his anger was incarnate.

"Every month there's an audience," the Jeweler explained, "and you have to be present for whatever might arise. Some are only looking for meds, or a job, or payback, but for others, he changes their lives with some little thing: Señor as their baby's godfather, or helping out with a quinceañera. He grants things to them all. And what was he supposed to do if someone asked for a corrido?"

The Artist nodded, suddenly both guilty and excited at the scene. The crowd at the back was a blur, an indistinct mass of gray, but he could clearly see those almost at the front of the line, who stood straight, tugged their hair to the side, kept quiet, did up a button. And at the head, surrounded by the Court, the King looked them each in the eye, listened to the favor requested, motioned to the Manager and the Manager made a note. Some he stroked their hair or counseled in a grave tone of voice. Then they wanted to kiss his hand or embrace his knees, and the King allowed them to adore him for a moment before casting them off with gentle force.

The Jeweler, too, was dazzled by the audience; he, so fine, seemed to flourish at the passion expressed by the simple; outside he likely would have looked straight through them, but here he didn't miss a trick when it came to seeing that Señor worked miracles, and they were transformed.

"That's why we're here," said the Jeweler, "to give him power. By ourselves, what good is any one of us? None at all. But in here, with him, with his blood, we're strong . . . And let no one think they can take anything from Señor!"

The Jeweler was almost shouting by the end, and the people cowered for a second, until the Journalist slapped him on the back.

"Easy, tiger, easy now."

The Artist tried to distract the Jeweler by asking, "You ever make special pieces for the people?"

"All my pieces are special," he replied, "and all the special pieces you see here were made by me."

For a second the Artist thought the Journalist and the Jeweler exchanged a look of surprise, or that the Journalist was about to fly off the handle, but it was only for an instant, because then the Audience ended.

The King rose and strode toward the hall, the people's pleading looks trickling down to his feet; behind him, the Manager consoled those still in line: Next month, next month.

"Come on," said the Journalist.

They rushed to the back of the royal entourage and the Journalist approached the King.

"Señor, it seems we have a problem with the Artist . . . "

The King stopped, arched an eyebrow.

"Well, not with the Artist, what problem would we have with him," the Journalist grinned, "it's the DJs who have the problem. They won't play his songs."

"Oh? And why's that?" said the King, as if to say, What's new.

"Same old story: they mustn't be seen speaking well of you to the people."

The King glanced back toward the Gallery, to where people were heading home, laden with favors.

"As if we need those asses in order for people to speak of me," he said. "Don't you worry about it, the Manager here will arrange things with our friends to move your music on the street . . . After all, isn't that the way we do business?"

The King looked tired, but also full of restrained power. He smiled, and his smile seemed a protective embrace that said to the Artist, Why sugarcoat the ears of those fuckers? We know what we are and we're good with it. Let them be scared, let the decent take offense. Put them to shame. Why else be an artist?

They're dead. All of them, dead. The others. They cough and
spit and sweat their deaths, rotted through with self-satisfied
deceit. As if they shat diamonds. They grin with bare teeth,
like corpses; like corpses, they figure nothing bad can happen
to them.

Word.

They have a nightmare, the others: the men here—the good
guys—are their nightmare; the smell here, the noise here,
the hustle here. But here it's more real, in the flesh, alive and
kicking, and them, they're not even close, nothing but bags
of bones, pappyjacks with no color. Pale reflections, lifeless
cut-outs, held up by pins.

You don't ask dead men for their say-so. Or at least not
dead shitbags. You just do what you do. You swagger and
you strut, you speak the name out loud, and don't take any
notice if it wigs the others out. Or you do: just to feel their
fear, right, because their fear is what you feed off and makes
clear that the flesh of the good is brave and necessary, that it
shakes things up and fills the space.

They should be snatched up by the hair and have their
faces rubbed in that vile truth, that ruthless putrid truthful
truth, let them be lured in by it. They should be stuck on the
spikes of our sun, drowned in the ruction of our nights, have

our songs inserted under their fingernails, be lain bare with our skins. They should be tanned and hided. And caned.

It spooks them to hear talk of their bad dream, which takes words and lives. It spooks them for One to be the sum of all their flesh, to have Him be as strong as all of them together. It spooks them to see who He is and what He's like and how He's named. They only dare to admit it when they abandon themselves to their truths, in juice, in dance, in heat, they're fucked, that's all they're good for. They'd rather hear just the pretty part, but the songs we sing don't ask their say-so, a corrido aint a painting that hangs on the wall to look pretty. It's a name and it's a weapon.

If it spooks them, cool.

Either way. In the end they'll find out they're nothing but maggoty flesh.

Softly, moving from one side of the roof to the other, head rising and dipping, the Artist sang his roughneck song about a rich lady who threw a party at her house. It got crashed by two little bigshots hoping to make their name in the business; looking smooth, the bucks slipped in and hooked a couple of stuckup honeys who were rich and well-to-do, which was the name of the song, "Rich and Well-to-Do", tho, the Artist acknowledged, it could also have been called "Luscious and in Love" or "Left in Love", or at least that's what he thought. So the bigshots started working their silverspoon ladies, using them as mules to cart junk here to there, and man was it perfect cause these girls loved to shake it, and they looked—went the song—like movie stars, tho they were really just corrido queens; thing is, it couldn't last forever, no, not a setup that sweet, because of course they really fell for it, the gear, the front, they wanted it all to come true and started sticking up their noses and watching who they went with, and what good were they then, if changing their ways meant leaving cash on the table? So, psh, what are you going to do? The bigshots stuck the girls on a bus, Be there in a flash, they said, y'all just get off round that bend, but no, no sir, next stop was the other end of the world, and they were sorry as they watched the bus pull out, but there wasn't nothing for it—a job's a job.

He'd struggled to smooth out the song's rough edges, especially at the end, when they realize they got to go it alone. But he had it down now, and once he had it he all of a sudden stopped and looked around the roof and took in the burning Kingdom with his eyes: the long strip of sand surrounding it, the acacia trees, the sky that raced and raced in all directions, one side still bright blue and the other flaming rose, and he thought: far as the eye can see, that's how far the King's reach extends, and with it, my words, and considering this quietly he added: Bastards.

The Artist stayed there until darkness began to eat up all the color, feeling so small and so free, and then he went down. He passed the area where the study was, close to the gallery, then the area where the games room was, skirted the wing where King's quarters lay, close to the terrace, and finally the guards' quarters and the girls' rooms. Though there were corridors he had yet to explore, he no longer struggled to find his way to the Girl in the Palace. She was going to love this song! The Girl hadn't wanted him to write about how when she was little she was sold for a clapped-out car, but with hooks like the ones in his corrido, she would surely see he was making amends for her, too.

He watched her folding clothes on the bed and it filled him with tenderness: her slight waist, her slender shoulders, the taut, pale skin that he'd been so excited to touch in the early days and that now made him want to comfort her and make her happy, even if he couldn't. He slid a finger down the pebbles of her spine. She turned and instead of surprise wore an expression that said Oh, you.

"Listen to what I wrote to get even."

He sang his corrido a cappella.

As he sang, the Artist slapped his thighs and made faces he hoped were witty, but when he saw the Girl's wrath he felt ridiculous. In the end, silence and more silence, brief but unyielding.

"You don't know jack, do you?" she said with scorn.

"What is it I should know?"

The Girl turned her back and kept folding. The Artist began to serenade her, circling as tho taking a stroll through the room. He was giving his best shot at getting the Girl to smile but she wouldn't even glance his way and he saw it was best to stop playing cute. So he kissed her shoulder and headed for the door.

"Come on, fool. What do you think?" she asked before the Artist made his exit, adding, "They're badass motherfuckers and you're nothing but a clown."

The Artist turned, perplexed more at the venom in the Girl's voice than her scorn for him or the way she insulted the King.

"I thought you were happy here."

"That's what we tell all our customers," she shot back bitterly. Then wheeled to face him and said, "Have you heard yourself recently? You talk like every other asshole around here. Making jewels." She jerked her chin up, challenging. "Now step off; I don't want to see you near my bed again."

The Doctor stopped prodding his eye sockets and said sullenly:

"If you refuse to let me examine your head with the proper instruments, I can't tell what the problem is . . . Though I have my suspicions."

This last line he added in a tone both harsh and sad. The Artist wouldn't let anyone near him with a knife or anything like one. They spent the next few seconds in silence: a dialogue of suppressed premonitions. Then the Doctor shook it off with a smile.

"What we can do, in the interim, is take care of the obvious problem." He bent over a desk and took out a box which he set down a few feet from the Artist. "Because it is obvious, even if not to you."

A pyramid of letters and numbers decreasing in size, down to tiny at the base. The Doctor said:

"I haven't used this for a long time; nobody here wants to wear specs. Cover one eye."

The Artist covered his left. The Doctor carried on.

"I'm surprised the courtiers don't spend all day running into each other in the corridors. Read me the letters you see."

"En, jay, gee, kay, three, tea, one, why, are, tea, pee."

"Though now that I think about it, there certainly are some run-ins, as I'm sure you've realized, eh? Next line, other eye."

"Aitch, oh, see, queue, doubleyou, en, zee, ex."

"Good. See, sometimes you get the impression that each man's got his own knife and fork now, altho no one should be thinking about a banquet. Next one, back to the left again."

"Jay, a, two, tea, ess, see, eight, a, zee, eff . . . bee?"

"Close: three. I wish things were like back in the day, but, between you and me, seems like everyone's lost it. Next line."

"Dee, e, why, e, one, are, vee, seven."

"El, not one. See, the Traitor's making deals with the crew from the south, but there's no way to know if that's because he's been told to by someone here. They're different down there, they're new at this, do things on the down low. Next."

"Jay, e, eff . . . ess again, three, why, nine, pee, doubleyou, four, dee."

"Hm. Here we go. So on the one hand, top dog is getting nervous, best not even to go near him when he's all het up like that, boy's been trigger-happy since he was a pipsqueak . . . And on the other, That Woman is there, and who knows what her angle is. Next."

"En, e . . . zee?, e, you, jay, el, en again."

"Tsk, tsk. That's enough. Time to dust this thing off."

The Doctor went back to his desk and pulled out a contraption full of glass slides and wires. He removed and replaced lenses and slid it over the Artist, on his nose. Suddenly the letters on the card were clear, but jumpy. They're jiggling, the Artist said. The Doctor switched lenses again. How bout now? Now they're slurred. More lens changing. Now? The Artist made no reply. He was no longer looking at the letters. The shock of so much new minutiae unsettled him: a slight crispness to the walls, gold dust dancing in the sun's rays. And suddenly: the Heir, standing there in the doorway.

"I *what?*" he asked.

The Artist couldn't help but notice his threads. And now, with these eyes, he saw better what they said: his pants linen not denim; soft, crème-colored shirt, not checkered, no stitching. Like the cut of the cloth revealed what the Heir was made of, told of a past different from the rest, more genteel days, troubled blood, a tense way of being there.

"Nothing. Just giving the Artist here a check-up," the Doctor replied.

The Heir smiled broadly, but it was like an accident on his face.

"Course you are. That's your job," he nodded slowly. "*Your* job, right? Yours and no one else's. Not the Witch's, for example."

He took a few steps in until he stood before the Doctor.

"What is that bitch trying to cure the King of?" He placed his hands on the Doctor's shoulder. "Tell me."

The Doctor met the Heir's gaze for a second, no more, and then his eyes quivered, watering.

"I don't know, I'm just a doctor, I don't know about that sort of thing."

"What sort of thing, Doc? Explain yourself, See, apparently I'm just a dumbfuck who imagines all kinds of stupid shit. A minute ago I thought you were talking about me, but I'm glad I was wrong, cause when I don't know what's going on, I get a little fucked off. So I prefer straight talk."

"I swear I don't know," the Doctor seemed to hunch over himself, a slight tremor rattling through him. "I'm not that close."

The Artist saw goosebumps rise on the Heir's neck, and the first thing he thought was that it was the sort of rage felt by a man with no game in the sack.

"Well, as soon as you find out, you let me know, because you and I *are* that close." He removed his hands and headed for the door. Before leaving, he added, "And don't worry: it's all a question of learning your place before it's too late."

Ever since the Girl kicked him out, the Artist had been bunking in the guards' quarters, slipping into the cot of whoever was on rounds. That night he'd been abruptly awakened by a guard just getting off, but sleep had forsaken him so he decided not to move to the newly abandoned bed. He began to wander through the Palace in search of a spot with enough light to reread the books of stories and poems on loan from the Journalist. Carrying them with him was like walking with a compadre who knew all manner of secrets.

He leaned over a balcony looking out over the courtyard, which had lights on all night, and picked out a garden bed. The Artist was about to head down and get comfortable when he heard the shouting.

"Where? Where?" The Witch appeared from one end, a walkie-talkie at one ear. From the other, just beneath him, emerged a guard, dragging the Commoner.

"Picked her up as she was trying to hitch a ride on a semi," said the guard, clearly overconfident. He stood, waiting. Perhaps thought this was when the Witch would thank him, but all she did was point to where he'd come from: Out. The guard left. The two women gazed at one another in silence for several seconds. Then the Commoner said:

"Those dogs can't go telling me whether I can leave."

The Witch executed a powerful arc with one hand, striking the Commoner down with her slap.

"It's not the dogs who are telling you. It's me."

She crouched, yanked her daughter up and ragdolled her shoulders.

"What the fuck are you trying to pull? Can't you see there is no other train? Is this what I waited so long for?"

She let her go with a weary look but then took her daughter's hands and, more sweetly, said:

"Do you know what's out there? Trash. Here, it's all going to be yours, soon as I fix that man. Sit tight a little longer. When the rich blood I give him puts his seed to rights, you've got to be ready, too. Even if his damn peacock doesn't work I'm going to find a way to leave all of this to you."

"When did I ever say I was interested in this dump?" the Commoner asked, head still bowed. Her mother stood. On doing so she saw the Artist watching, but showed no surprise.

"I didn't see you turn your nose up at it either," she said, "so if you ask me, you are interested. And even if you're not, we're in it up to our necks."

She lifted the Commoner up by one arm, and as she pulled her towards their rooms cast a quick glance back at the Artist.

"You are not going to fuck things up," she said. "No way am I going to let it all be ruined by some deadbeat."

He went with her back to the City.

"I know how to get out without being seen," he told her, and tho he knew it was playing with fire, the way her eyes lit up gave him the confidence to continue. She wanted out so bad she didn't even ask why he offered to escort her.

The Artist led her to the end of one of the gardens and they leapt the fence at a spot he'd seen on a walk where it wasn't electrified because a stream ran beneath.

When they got to the City, the Commoner led him by the hand, as tho he were the one needing to be shown around the cantinas by the bridge. With fairground glee she showed him cherished sights in each one: a jukebox old as dirt, a turtle-eyed barkeep, a wooden bar carved with cuss words, a band whose members were all midgets, a bathroom where women stood to pee. And at places she'd never been to, she still walked in as tho to size up the tables, holding the Artist's sleeve in silence.

The Artist saw pass before his eyes the world that by the belt he'd learned to survive, and could not share the Commoner's delight. He did see new things, tho, or perhaps the same things were revealed with new force, as if he'd had a callus skinned off his eye and now the whole of him absorbed details he'd never before perceived, things that had been blurred like a bad photo. He picked up on the wounded pluck of the girls who worked it solo and the apathy of pimped old pros; he understood the cold felt by the old codger on the floor, moaning but unable to ask for anything; and a sign for a lost little girl brought home the horror of being tortured by cowards. He recognized himself in an ashen boy coaxing squalid notes from a trumpet but could tell this kid had it worse than he ever did, because he had a littler one to look after, curled up on his back. The Artist had never had to look after anyone else.

It's as if there is no right to beauty, he thought, and thought that the city ought to be set alight from its foundations, because in each and every place where life sprouted up through the cracks, it was immediately abused. But then he looked at the Commoner, who stood on the sidewalk, gazing at a hooker without being seen, contemplating the girl as tho embracing her with her eyes, as tho consoling her, and the Artist thought that for an instant, a light more pure was cast down on the slum, and he was privileged to be able to see it.

"Haven't seen you round the way of late, sugarpie," said a voice behind him. "Months. Thought maybe you didn't like what I gave you."

The Artist turned and saw a big-belly flab man, who fingered his belt buckle as he spoke. The Commoner seemed at first to be scared and then to be pissed: her whole body recoiled as tho ready to spring, but all she did was take one step over and stand by the Artist. The man, too, took a step— forward, toward them.

"So . . . how bout a deal? You know, each give the other what they want."

Though he was instantly overcome with fury, the Artist had no idea how to defend anyone and put his hands behind his back to tuck his shirt in, just to do something, as tho gearing up to fight. The man backed up and cactus-armed in fear.

"Hey, hey! Easy, amigo, no need to go taking out your piece. You want her, take her, girls like this are a dime a dozen."

The Commoner wrapped her arms around the Artist from behind and pulled him to the door of a building without letting go of his chest. She shouted an obscenity at the man and then she and the Artist took backward steps, as if entrenching themselves against the city, until they made it through the door. Of the hotel. It was a hotel. They stood a few seconds staring at reception unsure of what to do, and then the Commoner approached the desk, requested a key, and signaled to the Artist to follow.

Once inside the room she undressed herself quickly and him furiously, and then mounted him—cold, focused—and the Artist was struck by something that made him feel miserable: he sensed that she was staring past his face, at the pillow, at the wall. That was why he simply placed his hands gently on her hips and waited. And suddenly she stopped, head bowed, still on top of him.

"I'm not going to apologize," she said, and slid off and lay beside him, "it's just that I don't know how to act with men who seem nice."

They lay in silence. A light bulb abuzz with mosquitoes stained the darkness. The Artist resolved to stop thinking, all he wanted was to be there with the Commoner. And suddenly he knew her blood: it was a faltering current, lurching clear of invisible boulders. The Artist pressed on a vein in the Commoner's arm and traced it to her wrist and back. He reached his other hand across her body and listened to the veins in one thigh. He traveled the skin that covered those fragile channels to the rhythm of her heart. He felt her blood begin to rush and felt his hands become useless, because every inch of her skin foretold another current, a bloodstream. The Artist gazed at her face: a deliberate face; there are faces that seem accidental, but not this face whose parts all rhymed, not this skin like hot sand that sculpted round cheekbones, tiny mouth, teeth biting a lip; not this face that now sang to itself. They loved one another like people lingering over every instant, with the certainty that it was the only way to be alive. And such lassitude, so slowly: no desire to reach the end of this line.

Afterward they walked outside as if enlightened, indifferent to the nonstop action on the street. Someone approached hawking bootleg CDs and the Artist saw that among them was one of his, which meant nothing. The King had kept his word, but this didn't move him. He'd learned more important things that day.

From a cantina they saw the Gringo emerge, staggering. He stared in surprise but betrayed no sense of scandal.

"I thought you were on the other side," said the Artist.

"Been and came back, but it was no use, they don't know jack. Pocho didn't go over anymore; once he turned his back on them, he did all his business on this side. Besides: only thing he was in charge of was getting girls for Señor, for all the good that did. But that," he held a clumsy finger to his lips, "is hush-hush, eh? You didn't see a thing . . . and I didn't

56

either. Didn't see you two here. Better that way. Better not to know, with the shit that's about to hit the fan."

An icy dust swept through the city. The Gringo halfturned, stumbling, zigzagged a few feet, and set his course for a cantina door.

What's out there? What lies beyond it all? Another world standing, face to the sun? A wave with edges rippling out after a stone hits the water? (Could life be a stone hitting the water?)

To see and see and see and not to see: there is no shape, only a tangled mess grown weary of itself. Arrogant face, deadbeat world.

What's out there? What lies beyond the walls of things?

Like this, like this, there's nothing.

Turn your back on this smug cut grass and choose your own mirror: raise it to your eyes and see:

A chilling glimmer, a tiny spiral asking for a chance, a secret obscured in its own dark light. The whole world can be seen in this mirror, each detail a reversible code. Pieces and more pieces falling over themselves asking to be touched, ever-changing skin.

"So tell me how you write a corrido," the Journalist said. "You just tell the story, that's all?"

The Artist knew how but had never articulated it, expertise was like underwear, something concealed out of modesty that you were almost unaware of. And yet now he felt confident enough to expound.

"The story tells itself, but you have to coax it," he replied, "you take one or two words and the others revolve around them, that's what holds it up. Cause if you're just saying what happened, why bother with a song? Corridos aren't only true; they're also beautiful and just. That's why they're so right for honoring Señor."

The Journalist nodded, but seemed unconvinced.

They were on the terrace, having coffee. The Artist was enjoying their chat, so unlike the shakedowns soon to come. He was mastering more and more words thanks to the books the Journalist had given him and refused to take back, even when the Artist insisted.

"That's good," the Journalist said, "that's good for us, the ones who polish his shoes and watch his back, but you're something else; not saying you don't mean it, but what you do is art, amigo, no need to use all your words of praise on Señor."

"Why not? I write about what moves me, and if what moves me are the things the Chief does, then why not?"

"Sure, sure, don't get me wrong, Artist, all I mean is that your thing has a life of its own, one that doesn't depend on all this. It's good that our hellraising serves as inspiration, I just hope you never have to choose. Seems to me like you're pure passion, and if one day you have to choose between your passion and your obligation, Artist, then you are truly fucked."

He felt the Journalist was plucking a chord he'd been hoping to keep quiet. So, cautious, he responded in a way that both concurred and offered resistance:

"Ffft, my songs will outlive me in the end."

The door to the room at the far end opened and there appeared the Witch. Her long white dress made the blood on her fingertips jump out. The whole of her tense, as tho her entire body were a loaded gun.

"What are you doing here?" she spat. "Don't you have any-place else to waste your time? Think you'll learn something here, digging in like nits? Asswipes. Piss off! Damn you, get out of here! There's nothing to see!"

The Journalist motioned vaguely and stood. The Artist got out of his chair, still bent almost double; frightened, because unlike the majority of the Palace bigwigs, the Witch had looked straight at him, and her eyes burned.

They headed for the guards' dining room. In silence at first, and then the Journalist, as tho feeling the need to apologize to a guest, confided:

"Not so long ago we were all tight, like family, but now, well, they say the alliance with that other boss fell through . . . Plus there's this war on the horizon . . . "

"But can't you go with them, try to set things straight?"

"Not me, a subordinate, no. There are those who can address the King, but I'm not the kind to jump my station." Somberly, he added, "Tho some are, Artist, that's for damn sure: there's that fool struck out on his own, or found himself a new boss, I'm starting to see."

In the dining room they ran into the Heir, who stood grabbing pieces of raw meat from a lone platter. He glanced up at the new arrivals from the far end of the long table, eyed them quickly but said nothing. The Heir brought pieces of meat to his mouth greedily, but with the slow self-assurance of a man who knows no one is going to fight him for a mouthful. They sat at the opposite end of the table as if to carry on with their conversation, but now said not a word.

That look he had, the fatherly affection, the innocence with which he said:

"There's no one I trust the way I trust you." And if that weren't enough, added: "There are those who will never be satisfied, plain and simple; you, on the other hand, know your place and are happy with your lot."

That look he had, attention focused solely on his object, certain that no one else deserved it at that instant; the look of complicity. The way he touched the Artist's shoulder and led him through the grounds to show off his peacock: the easy intimacy, here we are, just you and me, discussing important things. And the cadence: such unflustered steps, the soles of his feet placed carefully on the ground the whole way. It all confirmed: the King speaks the truth. Which one? He was needed, the Artist was to slip into a baptism party nearby, where one of the King's enemies would be. The Artist, much as it would trouble him, was to pass himself off as a dissident and find out if anyone was conspiring from within. The Artist couldn't tell a soul, because—eyes sincere, insisting—he alone could be trusted, and he alone, given his talent, could pull it off. The Artist embraced his mission with faith and honor, even if he did have to shuttle to one corner his doubts about the last thing the King said, which lingered on like background buzz.

"Time has come for you to make yourself useful, Artist."

So he returned once more to the grimy streets of yore. He knew how to keep his mission under wraps as he searched for the rival top dog to sneak him into the reception. No one beat the Artist at the art of being unseen. All he had to do was prick up his ears and circle the word on the street like a buzzard above a dying man, until he found his way to the right joint.

He approached the top dog after watching him for three days, clocking his habits and noting he had a thing for call girls, that he tried to entice them with song. The Artist laid systematic siege, awaiting the exact moment when the dog was feeling fly; not only did the Artist know the requested tune but had prepared a little bonus, set to impress: an easy corrido, puffed up and swaggering, exalting the exploits he'd heard about the guy.

"Not bad, ace," said the top dog, trying not to let on that he'd liked the song, "but tell me: you already got someone to flatter, no?"

"Used to, but that place is going from bad to worse, truth is I'm looking to make a move."

"That a fact? Don't try me on, cause I can spot a bigmouth a mile off."

The Artist puckered his lips, pooched them out, and said, "Go ahead, search mine."

The punk laughed and feted the joke with much table-slapping.

"Hooo! If it's true you're just a singer, long as your voice don't dry up, it's all good. I'll take you to my boss, like a present. Can you write him a song?"

The Artist wrote more than one, he wrote corridos of friendship for the enemy capo, so fawning they seemed to say he was the true king. Fortunately, they didn't ask for any that criticized the King, but even singing for the other man made something between the Artist's belly and chest burn, a kind of pain he didn't recognize; to keep it from turning him sour he kept telling himself that to lie for Him was worth it, it was.

He plowed gently through the party, sure of where to stand, who to mark, when to speak. He had it down. This party, too, had its jangling gold, its blondes, its red anteater boots, had a band on a stand and a roast, had plenty of hooch, guards, a priest in its pocket. And the Artist set out to find the tête-à-tête that would let him in on the scheming. There were many: the old man scheming against his wife, three girls scheming against their bridesmaid dresses, two roughnecks against a moneyman, a priest against his urge to down the *sotol*; but none led him out of the dark. It was all just like the Court.

The Artist looked and looked with the specs the Doc had sent him, and what jumped out at him was this: *it was all the same.* He could feel the fiesta dribbling by him at the rate of routine. The only odd one there was him, who was seeing it all from outside. The only *special* one was him. It was so beautiful to see that, like a soft glow among the people, like the feeling that things get better when you walk into the room. And as he sang his corridos for the other king, a lightskinned cat lacking grace but sporting tux, the Artist was so smooth that it should have scared him to see how easy it was to feel at home in the role of a man with no blood debt. And there, at that moment, the buzz that had been troubling him since the King's command disappeared. The King's face appeared to him in all its detail, as if under a magnifying glass, and he saw how flaccid the skin, how precarious his constitution, like that of anyone here in this place. He pretended not to be thunderstruck by the discovery. He decided to leave, but before finding the exit had the wherewithal to pick up on a man talking at the bar, whom he examined carefully for a fraction of a second, enough to take in his fine suit, enough to realize that it was the same dog from the newspaper photos in the library, always beside the other man, equally as elegant.

The music cranked up all at once, right from the getgo, with the first *ay*, and then the voice carried the melody, the bass bumped up and down as if spellbound by the beat, the accordion swooped down low on the verses and sped up at the curves; and all the while the drum, solemn, held its own.

Ay, this is a sad corrido
That tells the story of my King
A man everybody envies
For his proud and noble reign

King, your man got whacked
They stuck a rod right through his crown
Smoked another with a gat
Seems to be the latest thing

Some dogs just want to leg it
And some conspire against you
Tho it's you who took them in
Gave them cash and loved them true

The boys that care bout you are down
Because they see you looking low
But we're all a family
And I won't let you go

They say you were real sick
Meanwhile your boys began to fight
But I don't think you ever said
You didn't need us in your life

Some dogs just want to run
While some conspire against you
Tho it's you who made them rich
Gave them peace and loved them true

Tho you don't say it, King, I know
You don't want us getting shot
Cause you're not made of stone
And we're the only sons you've got

He's our father and a King
And I swear to you he's good
On his turf you damn well best
Be working for the kingdom

Some kingdom cons just want to run
While some conspire against you
Cause you gave them more than cash
You gave them your ambition too

He scribbled the lyrics furiously almost the moment he left
the reception, leaning against the bar in a cantina. And before
passing his new corrido on to his colleagues, the Artist felt the
kind of sparks that fly when you hurtle downhill in a truck;
and felt as if he'd let something go.

On his way back to the Palace he asked himself what would happen if he simply turned another way, any way that wasn't the one he already knew. Ever since arriving at Court he'd been surprised by people's urge to cross the line, or to go to some other city, even if it was on this side. Not even tales of artists living the gringo life had altered his own Why would I go? stance, when the Palace had it all: voices, colors, drama, stories. And it wasn't that he'd changed his mind now, but that he admitted the possibility of there existing some point on the horizon that might be different from the two extremes he was bouncing back and forth between. What if . . . ? Why waste his time, he thought: one of the things he'd learned is that you stay where you're told, until you feel it's no longer your place.

He returned and knew right away there had been another tragedy, tho this time not because people rushed to the scene of the crime but because they rushed away from it, with more haste than fear, and that was truly awful. He made his way against the tide to the main courtyard. Right in the middle he saw, at first, simply a pool of blood over which the Doctor was bent, but as he approached he began to distinguish the soaking red silhouette of a man whose arms and legs were splayed, and then he recognized it as the body of the Journalist. Rage hurtled to his balled fists; this was the first time he'd lost a friend, despite never having called him that. Those motherfuckers, he said, chewing the words. The Journalist had had his throat slit clear across and was gazing up at the sky as if expecting to see someone pass. Next to his head was the flick he'd been killed with: a dagger, again, with a curved blade.

"Motherfuckers," the Artist repeated, "this time they made it all the way in."

As soon as he said it, something else popped into his head, tho he tried to push it out: I wish.

The Jeweler approached, running clumsily, looking shocked. When he got there he bent over the weapon.

The Doctor looked perplexed.

"What I don't get is what they're playing at, killing with a knife; it's grotesque."

"This wasn't the same dogs."

"How do you know?"

"This knife is different, this knife is a piece of shit."

With the speed of the subconscious, the Artist saw who shot Pocho and the Journalist and why and decided he could no longer carry on as an outside observer. He left the courtyard without a word, because now, in addition to rage, finally he felt fear. He went to find the Commoner, the Commoner, where was she? Not in her room, not in the garden, not in the corridors, not on the terrace.

"You've been with my daughter."

The Witch confronted him, suddenly there on the terrace without warning. She observed him closely, tho without the customary fury. She had made her proclamation with chilling self-possession. The Artist was amazed at how different she seemed, it was as if she'd resolved some great dilemma and were finally concerning herself with trivialities.

"Did you get her pregnant?"

The Artist instinctively said No, unable to conceive the other possibility.

"You ought to know," she continued, and held out a piece of paper on which were scribbled large, unsteady letters.

"Your girls no good to you now shes nokt up ask the singer," the note said. The Artist couldn't help but be touched when he saw the penmanship: he'd been the one to teach the Girl to trace letters and now he wondered why she would lie. Only afterward, all at once, was he struck by the possibility that it was true, and then he got vertigo. The note trembled in his hands. The Witch took it and stroked the Artist's face.

"It's okay, just keep this quiet and we'll take care of it."

She gazed at him with a tenderness he recognized but couldn't place, then turned and walked out.

He ran to the Girl's room simply to confirm that the only traces of her were a couple of left-behind dresses. Then, frantic, he set out once more through the Palace in search of the Commoner, his urgency increasing with each empty room. Not only did he know what the Witch was capable of, he also felt the need to prevent anything more from happening.

He found her in the games room. She was playing solitaire at a card table, and when he walked in she hardly even glanced up, absent.

"Is it true?" he asked.

She seemed to startle and wrinkled her forehead. What?

Of course not. No. It couldn't be true. Or at least the Girl couldn't have known. But the seed was already planted and

70

the solution began to take shape. He pulled the Commoner gently up by the arm. Without much conviction, she tried to shake him off.

"What's wrong? What do you want?"

"Nothing," the Artist replied. "Just let me show you someplace."

The Artist led her from the Palace and she put up no fight nor showed any enthusiasm. He took her to a hotel far from the street, by the bridge, and told her he'd be back for her tomorrow, to wait for him. On his way out, a smell on the street made him recall which kind of tenderness the Witch had shown: he'd seen the way people pet lambs before a sacrifice.

When, the next day, he was told that the King was waiting in the library, the Artist got an inkling: he was about to be let in on a secret; electrified, he intuited that the relationship between them had entered new territory, a tighter place, where they shared a more complete view of the world that allowed mirrors like the one the Artist had constructed to be exchanged.

"He's already been told about your latest song," said the Manager, but the Artist was unable to read his face and see if he'd liked it or not. He now got an inkling, intuited a reprimand from the King, but then dismissed it, because once he told him what he'd seen at the party it would prove he was still on his side. The Artist even brought his accordion along so that afterward he could play him the song already circulating throughout the slums, in person.

The King was bent over the wooden table, palms on several outspread papers. He appeared not to be reading any of them, looked at them as tho searching for something specific, or measuring them. It seemed to the Artist as if his arms were the only still-strong thing about the King, as if the rest of his body were sinking into the floor with the force of its own gravity. The Artist upsidedown read one of the papers' headlines. "The Net Tightens", it said, with a photo of the King.

He had to tell him about the party, and wanted to sing him his song, but before he articulated anything at all the King lifted his gaze and said:

"So I'm a no-account fool? That's what you say? That I can't . . . "

He fell silent. The unfinished sentence and the fact that for the first time he'd addressed him not as usted but as tú suggested, yes, that there was some new bond between them, but not the one the Artist had hoped for.

"To get where I am, it's not enough to be a badass, right. You have to *be* one and you have to *look* like one. And I am, fuck knows I am," he paused, the Artist felt the King's voice teeter between wracking sob and fit of rage, "but I need my people to believe it, and *that*, you little shit, is your job. Not running around claiming that I . . . "

His body shook as tho every bone were dying to hightail it out of there.

"Señor, I thought . . . "

"Where the fuck did you get the idea that you could think? Where? You're a piece of fluff, a fucking music box, a thing that gets smashed, you piece of shit."

He took two steps toward the Artist, snatched his accordion, hurled it against one of the empty bookshelves and then kicked until keys and springs were scattered all over the room. His back to the Artist, fists clenched, he said:

"Still, it's my fault; that's what I get for playing with strays that bite."

The Artist knew that, following this, the King would turn and shred him, and knew that he would have the guts neither to make a stand nor to flee.

73

The Manager appeared all at once, almost between them, and announced:

"Señor, they're here."

The King glanced at the door to the boardroom, where a handful of green uniforms with yellow stars were taking a seat; he inhaled deeply, smoothed his hair gracelessly and walked to the room with the most timid steps the Artist had seen him take. The enemy, one of the enemies, was there, on his turf, and Señor was in anguish as if those men were of his ilk, or *as if they were the ones in charge.* The Manager closed the door behind him. The Artist heard the scraping of chairs and of the King, repeating: General, General, and then saying:

"We'll find a way around this, you'll see."

And then, nothing; but it was a condensed kind of nothing, one with texture, a nothing in which the Artist discerned an unsatisfied pause from the King, as if he couldn't carry on until he'd settled. He heard him call one of his guards, heard the guard's steps approach the head of the rectangular table and then sensed an even more informative nothing. In the time between the guard's final step and his Yessir, there was just enough time for the King to condemn him. Go jack the fucker up, he said to his soldier. That was what that nothing sounded like. Maybe the Artist could guess his words or maybe it was nothing but a surge of adrenalin that set his intuition on edge, but he lifted his feet from the floor and was off like a shot the instant the door handle began to turn, headed who knew where, with a determination he didn't know he had.

He bolted down hallways and through rooms that passed swiftly before his eyes because the Artist could hear the footsteps, clack, clack, clack of the goon behind him and urged his legs on with no sense of direction, or with some unfathomable compass that led him without warning to a blindspot. The balcony. The balcony and what lay beyond: the abyss of the desert. Or: the room that was not to be entered. Clack, clack, clack, clack comes the goon. He gripped the handle knowing that there was no hope, but the handle turned. He entered the room, stood at the center, stared at walls covered with paintings of women whose eyes seemed to follow whoever looked their way; all of them, the nude, the seated, the reclining, and those standing stiff. The Artist had seen the King enter and not exit before, knew there had to be a passageway. He quickly scanned the room and found, behind a full-length portrait, a crack, a vertical black line. Someone must have slipped out for a second and left the room unlocked. Clack, clack, clack, he heard the soldier almost outside. The Artist moved the painting: there really was a door. He slipped through and shut it behind himself, black-tar darkness flooding the space. Feeling along the walls he discovered he was in a tunnel, his stumbling feet told him he was descending short, broad steps. As he advanced, a tenuous orange glow began to light his way.

The glow became a glare and the Artist arrived in another room in which he found candles in every corner, an altar, necklaces of maguey thorns, crowns of peyote, blue feathers with bloody tips, a portrait of the Holy Bandit, stones on the floor in the outline of a man, earthenware jugs overflowing with water. He slowly raised his hands, as tho afraid to shatter the image. Then he heard footsteps descending, but not the boots of his pursuer, these steps were lighter and not as swift.

And there appeared the Witch. She stopped at the end of the room with a candle in each hand. Then, staring at the Artist all the while, *acknowledging* him all the while, she stepped up to the altar.

"Have you seen my daughter?" she asked.

"She's gone."

"Is she pregnant?"

The Artist shook his head. The Witch lowered her gaze, pensive; she seemed first disappointed, then simply resigned. She placed the candles on the altar, scanning it carefully, and then looked around as tho she'd lost something.

"Who would have thought such a sorry-ass stray could fuck everything up so royally. Fine mess you made. Not only do you not help me with the baby but you tell the whole world he'll never have a child. That was all it took for them to eat him alive." And then, as if speaking to herself, she added, "If only you hadn't let my daughter get away, that other bastard might've been interested, now that he can stop pretending he's not a threat and think about his own lineage."

Suddenly the Witch lost the thread that had been holding her together: the Artist glimpsed her endless exhaustion, a fatigue he'd have thought impossible. Sadly, she asked:

"Do you know where she went?"

"No."

"Well, good luck to her, maybe she'll find an easier path." She straightened her shoulders, pulled herself together and said, "But the rest of us have still got to live here."

She left. Moments later, the Artist followed. He stepped quietly, crouched on reaching the exit tho it wasn't necessary: the Palace was deserted. Magnificent and glacial as a royal tomb. He decided to escape through a back garden, but when he was on his way out bumped smack into the Jeweler, who held a curved-blade dagger in one hand, identical, of course, to that of the first murder. Blood dripped onto the white marble.

"It was no use," the Jeweler said through his tears, "no one helped him. Now what are we going to do?"

The Artist wished that the man was not carrying a knife, not because he thought the Jeweler might hurt him but because he held it as tho it were all he had left. The Artist sensed that if he attempted to help, he'd end up in the same state. He stepped cautiously to the side to pass the knife-wielding ghost of a man and went out to the grounds.

Tho he almost tripped over the body, he hardly registered the lifeless peacock, its throat slit, as he left.

It was because he now sensed he had all the time in the world that he didn't hurl his anxieties onto the Commoner, but also because since arriving at the hotel he'd been lost, for hours, in the contemplation of the new splendor she possessed. She said nothing, the Commoner, just smiled with newborn serenity, and her body, her entire body, breathed pure, from within an aura that the Artist was afraid to defile. Like a blossom, a thing different from whatever it was he was, generating her own energy, lifeblood. Amazing, he thought; women are something else, and all you have to do is get over yourself to see how they shine.

A miracle, he felt, that a woman like her could be contemplated for hours and hours by someone like him. That was what was called a miracle. Miracle, he murmured, and was tormented by the sense that something was wrong, a chorus repeating: what gave him the right, he was taking something that wasn't his, something intended for the one who'd helped him. The notion almost broke him for a moment but then something exploded inside and brought to his lips the word No: No, he cannot rule my life. No, I will not let them tell me what to do. It was a truth he knew already, deep down, though he'd been unable to name it. The revelation made him drop to the bed. He sat there quite some time, feeling the space around him expand, and feeling with each heartbeat how the Commoner could fill it.

In the middle of the night the Artist crept out of the room. He walked to the cantina where he'd first met the King, a port like any other: lots of people passing through and a handful of faithful standbys to keep it afloat. Always the walls were dripping with dark sweat, cigarette butts lost in the sawdust like grass. The only things that looked new were the streamers, at night there were always paper streamers, and music all day, except during the brief torpor that fell when the sun was vertical. Between songs he took in the banter of the B girls and admired the customers, who could be told apart from the simple drunks by their civility: May I? And he heard the fortunes and tragedies of the average jack:

The wetback who'd been deported by immigration and was unwanted on this side as well. They'd told him to sing the anthem, explain what a molcajete was and recite the ingredients of pipián to see if he was really allowed to stay; his jitters made him forget it all so they kicked him out too. The narco-in-training who sent bindles of smack over the river with a slingshot and then simply crossed over to pick them up, until one day he got a wild hair and hit a gringo in the head with his whiterock crackshot, and tho that was the end of his business, he still got a kick out of calling himself an avenger. The woman who, to free herself of her cheating husband, sold the house to a much-feared loanshark and left hubby with no house, no wife, and no peace. The boy who faked his own kidnapping to wheedle money from his parents, who believed the ransom note was real and replied, You know what? We're tired of that bum, how about bumping him off for half the price? And the boy, out of utter sorrow, said Okay, collected the cash, spent it on booze and then kept his word.

Who was the King? An allpowerful. A ray of light who had lit up the margins because it couldn't be any other way as long as it wasn't revealed what he was. A sad sack, a man betrayed. A single drop in the sea of men with stories. A man with no power over the terse fabric inside the artist's head. (The Artist allowed himself to feel the power of an order different from that of the Court, the skill with which he detached words from things and created his own sovereign texture and volume. A separate reality.)

To say homeboy, daydream, decanter, meadowland, rhythm.
To say anything.
 To listen to the sum of every silence.
 To give a name to the space full of promise.
 And then to fall silent.

It was all a matter of adding one plus one, stacking one stone on top of another to answer all the questions. He could have done it, and explained the whole thing to everyone, but this seemed so tedious, and he realized that he had absolutely no interest in exposing the intrigue—simply a series of incidentals exemplifying a system he now saw through.

That was what the Artist thought as he looked at a newspaper, one brought in by a new arrival who'd come at first light: there were two photos on the front page: in one, the Witch's body, peppered with countless bullet holes, dumped in with the Traitor's body, a shot to the back of the head. In the other, the King surrounded by five self-satisfied soldiers. It shook him to know the private realities behind the pictures. The vehemence that the Witch's inert body could never again express. The hidden imbroglios behind the fallen man. And there was something strange in the King's face, strange because it was out of place: he radiated satisfaction, the vanity of untouched grandeur. How did he do it? The Artist read in the caption at the bottom of the photo that the King had been captured during "an intimate encounter" with three women. Right, he thought. There's a story to be sung, not the role the King had played with grace until the end, but the other tale, the one about masks, and egotism, and misery. And then he said to himself: A story for someone else to sing. Why should he refute the paper's cock and bull? At this stage he preferred the truth over the true story.

A sudden silence at the Port made him scan the tables and couples to discover what was going on. What he saw at the entrance startled him not because it was a surprise but precisely because it was so logical: it had to happen, and it hadn't occurred to him. Here came the Manager, flanked by two guards. The elegance of the former and stiffness of the latter were not only out of place in the cantina but asserted a supremacy that the crowd sensed in an instant. The Artist decided to let them come up and kill him and, more than fear, felt sadness at no longer being able to undertake all the things that in the past few hours he had glimpsed. The Manager stopped in front of him, looked over at the band and ordered: Keep playing. Gently he pushed the Artist by the forearm to one end of the bar.

"Why so far from your friends, Artist?"

"These are my friends."

With scorn the Manager eyed the couples and musicians the Artist had motioned toward.

"Cut the shit." He pointed to the Traitor's photo in the paper. "That happened to him cause he was a spent cartridge, but you're still useful. Señor wants you to come work for him."

"Señor . . . ? Who . . . ?"

"Who do you think? The man it was always meant to be."

The Artist considered it for a second and realized immediately that even if he accepted, he could never write anything to sing the Heir's praises; he seemed a man whose soul was too puckered, and the Artist no longer had eyes for people like that. If this was it, if this was his last song, so be it, at least he'd figured out a few things out before it was all over.

"I hope you'll forgive me, Manager, but I can't give what I haven't got. I'm no good for what your Señor wants, so if there's nothing else, I think I'll go my own way."

The Manager's eyes bored into him, searching for sincerity. Then he turned back to look at the Port, made a face like he wanted to spit, and he spat. It was what everyone did, but the Manager's spit had airs.

"Fine," he said then. "Your loss. Because God knows things are going to run smooth now that we're all on the same side."

He gazed at the Artist one last time, hoping, perhaps, that he'd change his mind, and then headed for the door. Before walking out, he said something to one of the guards. The guard came back to the bar, opened his jacket with one hand and let the Artist see the piece between his belly and his belt; but rather than reach for it, his hand dipped into a pocket, pulled out a bill and slipped it to the Artist.

"This is good for one thing. Get on a bus and don't come back."

The Artist watched the last guard leave and sensed that the swinging of the doors carved a final notch on his wall too. From here on out, no king named his months.

The morning sun's glare knifed his eyes the second he stepped out of the cantina and his head began pounding once more.

Back at the hotel, She was sitting on the sheets, back to the light. Staring at her own motionless shadow. Lobo watched her from the halflight. Calm. A gentle rhythm about her. But also an uneasiness that traced a hint of sorrow on her lips. And what could he tell her? Not to worry, that it would all be all right? No, but how to tell her what he knew? Mentally he stammered out a few slick sentences and realized that was no way to deliver terrible news. Lobo crossed the room and stood beside her.

"Your mother is dead."

She stared in disbelief for a second. When she realized he wasn't lying she broke into sobs and collapsed on the bed; she covered her face with her hands and wept tears of utter solitude. Lobo stroked and stroked, as if to burnish away her pain. He could do it his whole life, soothe her daybreak. Gradually, her sobbing died down and She appeared to sleep. Then all of a sudden sat up, wiped her face and said:

"We have to go, we have to get out of here."

They gathered their things and set out into the city. From one day to the next the seasons had changed and a dense, golden pollen floated in the air, but She walked quickly, as tho to flee the dust of younger days, as tho to avoid anything that might tie her down.

He waited as She bought the tickets. They ran to the bus and there, at the bottom of the steps, She stopped him:

"You can't come now," She said, "I'm not saying you should wait for me, I'm not promising anything, but you can't come now."

She gave him a long kiss, and then Lobo felt it but said nothing, he knew he couldn't stop her. He let her hand slip through his and watched her go.

Pain hammered his temples but he did not curse it. It was his. If it was death, it was his. He owned every part of himself, of his words, of the city he no longer had to find, of his love, and his patience, and the determination to return to her blood, in which, like a wellspring, he'd recognized his own.

SIGNS PRECEDING
THE END
OF THE WORLD

For my Grandmother Nina, my Aunt Esther,
and my Uncle Miguel, on their way.

1

THE EARTH

I'm dead, Makina said to herself when everything lurched: a
man with a cane was crossing the street, a dull groan suddenly
surged through the asphalt, the man stood still as if waiting
for someone to repeat the question and then the earth opened
up beneath his feet: it swallowed the man, and with him a car
and a dog, all the oxygen around and even the screams of
passers-by. I'm dead, Makina said to herself, and hardly had
she said it than her whole body began to contest that verdict
and she flailed her feet frantically backward, each step mere
inches from the sinkhole, until the precipice settled into a
perfect circle and Makina was saved.

Slippery bitch of a city, she said to herself. Always about
to sink back into the cellar.

This was the first time the earth's insanity had affected her.
The Little Town was riddled with bullet holes and tunnels
bored by five centuries of voracious silver lust, and from time
to time some poor soul accidentally discovered just what
a half-assed job they'd done of covering them over. A few
houses had already been sent packing to the underworld, as
had a soccer pitch and half an empty school. These things
always happen to someone else, until they happen to you, she
thought. She had a quick peek over the precipice, empathized

with the poor soul on his way to hell. Happy trails, she said
without irony, and then muttered Best be on with my errand.

Her mother, Cora, had called her and said Go and take this
paper to your brother. I don't like to send you, child, but who
else can I trust it to, a man? Then she hugged her and held
her there on her lap, without drama or tears, simply because
that's what Cora did: even if you were two steps away it was
always as if you were on her lap, snuggled between her brown
bosoms, in the shade of her fat, wide neck; she only had to
speak to you for you to feel completely safe. And she'd said
Go to the Little Town, talk to the top dogs, make nice and
they'll lend a hand with the trip.

She had no reason to go see Mr. Double-U first, but a longing
for water led her to the steam where he spent his time. She
could feel the earth all the way under her nails as though
she'd been the one to go down the hole.

The sentry was a proud, sanguine boy who Makina had
once shucked. It had happened in the awkward way those
things so often do, but since men, all of them, are convinced
that they're such straight shooters, and since it was clear that
with her he'd misfired, from then on the boy hung his head
whenever he ran into her. Makina strolled past him and he
came out of his booth as if to say No one gets through, or
rather Not you, you're not getting through, but his impulse
lasted all of three seconds, because she didn't stop and he
didn't dare say any of those things and could only raise his
eyes authoritatively once she'd already gone by and was
entering the Turkish baths.

Mr. Double-U was a joyful sight to see, all pale roundness furrowed with tiny blue veins; Mr. Double-U stayed in the steam room. The pages of the morning paper were plastered to the tiles and Mr. Double-U peeled them back one by one as he progressed in his reading. He looked at Makina, unsurprised. What's up, he said. Beer? Yeah, Makina said. Mr. Double-U grabbed a beer from a bucket of ice at his feet, popped the top with his hand and passed it to her. They each uptipped the bottle and drank it all down, as if it were a contest. Then in silence they enjoyed the scuffle between the water inside and the water outside.

So how's the old lady? Mr. Double-U inquired.

A long time ago, Cora had helped Mr. Double-U out; Makina didn't know what had happened exactly, just that at the time Mr. Double-U was on the run and Cora had hidden him till the storm blew over. Ever since then, whatever Cora said was law.

Oh, you know. Alive, as she likes to say.

Mr. Double-U nodded, and then Makina added She's sending me on an assignment, and indicated a cardinal point.

Off to the other side? Mr. Double-U asked. Makina nodded yes.

Ok, go, and I'll send word; once you're there my man will get you across.

Who?

He'll know you.

They sat in silence once more. Makina thought she could hear all the water in her body making its way through her skin to the surface. It was nice, and she'd always enjoyed her silences with Mr. Double-U, ever since she first met him back when he was a scared, skinny animal she brought pulque and jerky to while he was in hiding. But she had to go, not just to do what she had to do, but because no matter how tight she was with him, she knew she wasn't allowed to be there. It was one thing to make an exception, and quite another to change the rules. She thanked him, Mr. Double-U said Don't mention it, child, and she versed.

She knew where to find Mr. Aitch but wasn't sure she'd be able to get in, even though she knew the guy guarding the entrance there, too: a hood whose honeyed words she'd spurned, but she knew what he was like. They said he'd offed a woman, among other things; left her by the side of the road in an oil drum on orders from Mr. Aitch. Makina had asked him if it was true back when he was courting her, and all he said was Who cares if I did or not, what counts is I please 'em all. Like it was funny.

She got to the place. *Pulquería Raskolnikova*, said the sign. Beneath it, the guard. This one she couldn't swish past, so she stopped in front and said Ask him if he'll see me. The guard stared back with glacial hatred and gave a nod, but didn't budge from the door; he stuck a piece of gum in his mouth, chewed it for a while, spat it out. He eyed Makina a little longer. Then turned half-heartedly, as though about to take a leak simply to pass the time, sauntered into the cantina, came back out and leaned against the wall. Still saying nothing. Makina snorted and only then did the guard drawl Are you going in or what?

Inside there were probably no more than five drunks. It was hard to tell for sure, because there was often one facedown in the sawdust. The place smelled, as it should, of piss and fermented fruit. In the back, a curtain separated the scum from the VIPs: though it was just a piece of cloth, no one entered the inner sanctum without permission. I don't have all day, Makina heard Mr. Aitch say.

She pulled the curtain aside and behind it found the bird-print shirt and glimmering gold that was Mr. Aitch playing dominoes with three of his thugs. His thugs all looked alike and none had a name as far as she knew, but not one lacked a gat. Thug .45 was on Mr. Aitch's side playing against the two Thugs .38. Mr. Aitch had three dominoes in his hand and glanced sidelong at Makina without setting them down. He wasn't going to invite her to sit.

You told my brother where to go to settle some business, said Makina. Now I'm off to find him.

Mr. Aitch clenched a fist around the bones and stared straight at her.

You gonna cross? he asked eagerly, though the answer was obvious. Makina said Yes.

Mr. Aitch smiled, sinister, with all the artlessness of a snake disguised as a man coiling around your legs. He shouted something in a tongue Makina didn't speak, and when the barman poked his head around the curtain said Some pulque for the young lady.

The barman's head disappeared and Mr. Aitch said Of course, young lady, of course . . . You're asking for my help, aren't you? Too proud to spell it out but you're asking me for help and I, look at me, I'm saying *Of course.*

Here came the hustle. Mr. Aitch was the type who couldn't see a mule without wanting a ride. Mr. Aitch smiled and smiled, but he was still a reptile in pants. Who knew what the deal was with this heavy and her mother. She knew they weren't speaking, but put it down to his top-dog hubris. Someone had spread that he and Cora were related, someone else that they had a hatchet to bury, though she'd never asked, because if Cora hadn't told her it was for a reason. But Makina could smell the evil in the air. Here came the hustle.

All I ask is that you deliver something for me, an itty bitty little thing, you just give it to a compadre and he'll be the one who tells you how to find your kin.

Mr. Aitch leaned over toward one of the .38 thugs and said something in his ear. The thug got up and versed from the VIP zone.

The barman reappeared with a dandy full of pulque.

I want pecan pulque, Makina said, and I want it cold, take this frothy shit away.

Perhaps she'd gone too far, but some insolence was called for. The barman looked at Mr. Aitch, who nodded, and he went off to get her a fresh cup.

The thug returned with a small packet wrapped in gold cloth, tiny really, just big enough to hold a couple of tamales, and gave it to Mr. Aitch, who took it in both hands.

Just one simple little thing I'm asking you to do, no call to turn chicken, eh?

Makina nodded and took hold of the packet, but Mr. Aitch didn't let go.

Knock back your pulque, he said, pointing to the barman who'd reappeared, glass at the ready. Makina slowly reached out a hand, drank the pecan pulque down to the dregs and felt its sweet earthiness gurgle in her guts.

Cheers, said Mr. Aitch. Only then did he let the bundle go.

· · ·

You don't lift other people's petticoats.

You don't stop to wonder about other people's business.

You don't decide which messages to deliver and which to let rot.

You are the door, not the one who walks through it.

Those were the rules Makina abided by and that was why she was respected in the Village. She ran the switchboard with the only phone for miles and miles around. It rang, she answered, they asked for so and so, she said I'll go get them, call back in a bit and your person will pick up, or I'll tell you what time you can find them. Sometimes they called from nearby villages and she answered them in native tongue or latin tongue. Sometimes, more and more these days, they called from the North; these were the ones who'd often already forgotten the local lingo, so she responded to them in their own new tongue. Makina spoke all three, and knew how to keep quiet in all three, too.

The last of the top dogs had a restaurant called Casino that only opened at night and the rest of the day was kept clear so the owner, Mr. Q, could read the papers alone at a table in the dining room, which had high ceilings, tall mullioned windows and gleaming floorboards. With Mr. Q Makina had her own backstory: two years before she'd worked as a messenger during emergency negotiations he and Mr. Aitch held to divvy up the mayoral candidates when their supporters were on the verge of hacking one another to pieces. Midnight messages to a jittery joe who had no hand in the backroom brokering and suddenly, on hearing the words Makina relayed (which she didn't understand, even if she understood), decided to pull out. An envelope slipped to a small-town cacique who went from reticent to diligent after a glance at the contents. Through her, the top dogs assured surrender here and sweet setups there, no bones about it; thus everything was resolved with discreet efficiency.

Mr. Q never resorted to violence—at least there was nobody who'd say he did—and he'd certainly never been heard to raise his voice. Anyhow, Makina had neither been naive nor lost any sleep blaming herself for the invention of politics; carrying messages was her way of having a hand in the world.

Casino was on a second floor, and the door downstairs was unguarded; why bother: who would dare? But Makina had no time to ask for an appointment and anyone who knew her knew she wasn't one to put people out for the sake of it. She'd already arranged for her crossing and how to find her brother, now she had to make sure there would be someone to help her back; she didn't want to stay there, nor have to endure what had happened to a friend who stayed away too long, maybe a day too long or an hour too long, at any rate long enough too long that when he came back it turned out that everything was still the same, but now somehow all different, or everything was similar but not the same: his mother was no longer his mother, his brothers and sisters were no longer his brothers and sisters, they were people with difficult names and improbable mannerisms, as if they'd been copied off an original that no longer existed; even the air, he said, warmed his chest in a different way.

She walked up the stairs, through the mirrored hall and into the room. Mr. Q was dressed, as usual, in black from neck to toe; there were two fans behind him and on the table a national paper, open to the politics. Beside it, a perfect white cup of black coffee. Mr. Q looked her in the eye as soon as Makina versed the mirrored hall, as if he'd been waiting for her, and when she stood before him he made a millimetric move with his head that meant Sit. A few seconds later, without being told, a smocked waiter approached with a cup of coffee for her.

I'm going to the Big Chilango, Makina said; no bush-beating for Mr. Q, no lengthy preambles or kowtows here: even if it seemed that skimming the news was downtime, that was where his world was at work; and she added On a bus, to take care of some family business.

You're going to cross, said Mr. Q. It wasn't a question. Of course not. Forget trying to figure out how he'd heard about it so fast.

You're going to cross, Mr. Q repeated, and this time it sounded like an order. You're going to cross and you're going to get your feet wet and you're going to be up against real roughnecks; you'll get desperate, of course, but you'll see wonders and in the end you'll find your brother, and even if you're sad, you'll wind up where you need to be. Once you arrive, there will be people to take care of everything you require.

He spoke each word very clearly, without stressing any, without moving a single muscle that wasn't strictly necessary. He stopped speaking and took one of Makina's hands, wrapped his fist around it and said This is your heart. Got it?

Mr. Q didn't blink. The light swept the steam from their coffee cups crossways, infusing the air with its bitter scent. Makina thanked him and versed out of there.

She stopped in the mirrored hall to think for a moment about what Mr. Q had said; sometimes she preferred the crass talk of Mr. Aitch, and certainly the slow celebratory tone with which Mr. Double-U spoke; but with Mr. Q nothing went to waste, it was always like pebbles were pouring from his lips, even if she didn't rightly know what each one was supposed to mean.

She looked into the mirrors: in front of her was her back: she looked behind but found only the never-ending front, curving forward, as if inviting her to step through its thresholds. If she crossed them all, eventually, after many bends, she'd reach the right place; but it was a place she didn't trust.

2

THE WATER CROSSING

She couldn't get lost. Every time she came to the Big Chilango she trod softly, because that was not the place she wanted to leave her mark, and she told herself repeatedly that she couldn't get lost, and by get lost she meant not a detour or a sidetrack but lost for real, lost forever in the hills of hills cementing the horizon; or lost in the awe of all the living flesh that had built and paid for palaces. That was why she chose to travel underground to the other bus depot. Trains ran around the entire circulatory system but never left the body; down there the heavy air would do her no harm, and she ran no risk of becoming captivated. And she mustn't get lost or captivated, too many people were waiting for her. Someone was covering her post at the switchboard while she was away, but only she spoke all three tongues and only she had mastered the poker face for bad news and the nonchalance with which certain names, oh, so long yearned for, had to be pronounced.

Most important were the ones awaiting her without caring what tongues she spoke or how she couriered. Her kid sister, who'd press close up beside her to eavesdrop on adult troubles, eyes round with attention, hands on knees. Makina could feel her absorbing the world, storing away the passions that came and went along the phone cord. *(Of course I still love you, Very soon, Any day now, Hold your horses, Did you get it? Did she tell you? When was that? How did it happen? How in the name of God is that possible? His name is so and so, Her name is such and such, Don't get me wrong, I never even dreamed, I don't live here anymore.)* She was growing up quickly, and in a man's world, and Makina wanted to educate her as to the essentials: how to take stock of them and how to put up with them; how to savor them. How even if they've got filthy mouths, they're fragile; and even if they're like little boys, they can really get under your skin.

And the boyfriend. A boyfriend she had and who she referred to that way though they'd never discussed it and she didn't feel like anyone's girl, but she called him her boyfriend because he acted so much like a boyfriend that not calling him so, at least to herself, would have been like denying him something written all over his face. A boyfriend. She'd shucked him for the first time back during the brouhaha about the mayors. The day it all ended Makina felt a little like getting wasted, but she didn't so much feel like liquor, it was more an itch to shake her body, so she'd been reckless and gone and shucked him as she had others on a couple of trips to the Little Town; what's more, it had been an entirely forgettable foray. And, no question, she'd shaken off the exhaustion of an ordeal that was now over; but even though she hadn't wanted to be fawned over, just wanted a man to lend himself, he had touched her with such reverence that it must have been smoldering inside him for ages.

She'd seen him before at the door of the elementary school where he worked, had noticed the way he wouldn't look at her, looking instead at every other thing around her; that was where she picked him up, sauntered over saying she needed a shawl so that he'd put his arms round her, took him for a stroll, laughed like a halfwit at everything he said, especially if it wasn't funny, and finally reeled him in on a line she was tugging from her bedroom. The man made love with a feverish surrender, sucked her nipples into new shapes, and when he came was consumed with tremors of sorrowful joy.

After that the man had gone to work in the Big Chilango, and when he came back months later he showed up at the switchboard to tell her something, looking so cocksure and so smart that she guessed what it was that he wanted to say and fixed it so she wouldn't be left alone with him. The man hovered in silence for hours on end until she said Come back another day, we'll talk. But when he came back she asked him about his gig and about his trip and never about what was going on inside. Then she asked him to stop coming to her work, said she'd seek him out instead. And she did: every weekend they'd shuck, and whenever she sensed he was about to declare himself, Makina would kiss him with extra-dirty lust just to keep his mouth shut. So she'd managed to put off defining things until the eve of the journey she was being sent on by Cora. Then, before she could silence him, he threw up his hands and though he didn't touch her she felt like he was hurling her from the other end of the room.

You're scared of me, he said. Not cause of something I did, just cause you want to be.

He'd stood and was facing her, straightening his sky-blue shirt; he was leaving without making love, but Makina didn't say anything because she saw how hard it had been for him to get up from the bed; she could play dumb—I don't know what you're talking about—or accuse him of making a scene, but the slight tremble betrayed by his lips, the bottled-up breathing of a man barely keeping his composure, inspired in her a respect that she couldn't dismiss; so she said It's not that, and he raised his head to look at her, the whole of him an empty space to be filled by whatever it was that Makina had to say, but she stammered We'll talk when I get back and then . . . Before she was through, he'd nodded as if to say Yeah, yeah, just sticking your tongue in my mouth again, and then turned and versed with the weariness of a man who knows he's being played and can't do a thing about it.

Three years earlier one of Mr. Aitch's thugs had turned up with some papers and told Makina that it said right there that they owned a little piece of land, over on the other side of the river, that a gentleman had left it to them. On the paper was a name that might have belonged to the man who had been her father before he disappeared a long time ago, but Makina took no notice and instead asked Cora what the deal was, what that was all about, and Cora said It's nothing, just Aitch up to his tricks. But in the meantime the thug took Makina's brother out drinking and washed his brain with *neutle* liquor and weasel words and that night her brother came home saying I'm off to claim what's ours. Makina tried to convince him that it was all just talk but he insisted Someone's got to fight for what's ours and I got the balls if you don't. Cora merely looked at him, fed up, and didn't say a word, until she saw him at the door with his rucksack full of odds and ends and said Let him go, let him learn to fend for himself with his own big balls, and he hesitated a moment before he versed, and in the doubt flickering in his eyes you could see he'd spent his whole life there like that, holding back his tears, but before letting them out he turned and versed and only ever came back in the form of two or three short notes he sent a long while later.

Two men ogled her in the bus ticket line, one pushed his face close as he passed and said Lucky's my middle name! He didn't brush against her but he felt her up with his breath, the son of a bitch. Makina wasn't used to that sort of thing. Not that she hadn't experienced it, she just hadn't let herself get used to it. She'd either tell them to fuck right off, or decide not to waste her time on such sad sacks; that's what she decided this time. But not because she was used to it. She bought her ticket and boarded the bus. A couple of minutes later she saw the two men get on. They were hardly more than kids, with their peach fuzz and journey pride. Since they probably had no notion of the way real adventures rough you up, they must've thought they were pretty slick adventurers. They jostled each other down the aisle to their seats, a few rows behind Makina's, but the one who had spoken to her came back and said with a smirk Think this is me, and sat down beside her. Makina made no reply. The bus pulled out; almost immediately Makina felt the first contact, real quick, as if by accident, but she knew that type of accident: the millimetric graze of her elbow prefaced ravenous manhandling. She sharpened her peripheral vision and prepared for what must come, if the idiot decided to persist. He did. Barely bothering to fake it, he dropped his left hand onto his own left leg, languidly letting it sag onto the seat and brush her thigh on the way back up, no harm intended, of course. Makina turned to him, stared into his eyes so he'd know that her next move was no accident, pressed a finger to her lips, shhhh, eh, and with the other hand yanked the middle finger of the hand he'd touched her with almost all the way back to an inch from the top of his wrist; it took her one second. The adventurer fell to his knees in pain, jammed into the tight space between his seat and the one in front, and opened his mouth to scream, but before the order reached his brain Makina had already insisted, finger to lips, shhhh, eh; she let him get used to the idea that a woman had jacked him up and then whispered, leaning close, I don't like being pawed by fucking strangers, if you can believe it.

The boy couldn't, judging by the way his eyes were bulging.

You crossing over to find a gig? Makina asked.

The boy nodded emphatically.

Then you'll need every finger you've got, won't you? Cause you can't cook or pick with your tootsies, now, can you?

The boy shook his head no less emphatically.

So, Makina continued. Listen up, I'm going to let you go and you're going to curl up with your little friend back there, and I swear on all your pain that if you even so much as think about me again, the only thing that hand's going to be good for is wiping ass.

The boy opened his mouth but now it was Makina who shook her head.

You believe me? she asked, and as she did so pressed his finger a little farther back. You don't believe me. You believe me?

Something in the boy's tears told Makina he believed her. She released him and watched as he staggered back to his seat. She heard him sniveling for a while and his friend going Holy shit, holy shit, holy shit, over and over; in the meantime she let herself be lulled by the sight of the gray city fleeing past in the opposite direction.

It was nighttime when she awoke. The boy's whimpering had stopped; all you could hear was the engine of the bus and the snoring of passengers. Makina could never be sure of what she'd dreamed, in the same way that she couldn't be sure a place was where the map said it was until she'd gotten there, but she had the feeling she'd dreamed of lost cities: literally, lost cities inside other lost cities, all ambulating over an impenetrable surface.

She looked out at the country mushrooming on the other side of the glass. She knew what it contained, its colors, the penury and the opulence, hazy memories of a less cynical time, villages emptied of men. But on contemplating the tense stillness of the night, the darkness dotted here and there with sparks, on sensing that insidious silence, she wondered, vaguely, what the hell might be festering out there: what grows and what rots when you're looking the other way. What's going to appear? she whispered to herself, pretending that as soon as they passed that lamppost, or that one, or that one, she'd see what it was that had been going on in the shadows. Maybe a whole slew of new things, maybe even some good things; or maybe not. Not even in make-believe did she get her hopes up too high.

.   .   .

The youngsters kept their distance the remainder of the trip. When the bus stopped at gas stations they waited for Makina to get off first and then cautiously emerged, like fugitives, and returned to their seats before she did. They crossed the entire country without one comment on the view.

Finally the bus reached the end of the land, at almost midnight the following day. A string of hotels facing the river was doing well off the mass exodus. Makina cruised around wondering how she'd find Mr. Double-U's contact, but couldn't discern any glance of recognition so decided to go into one of the hotels. She asked for a bed, paid, and they pointed to a door on the first floor but gave her no key. On entering she saw why. It was a very sizeable room with fifteen or twenty bunks on which were piled people of many tongues: girls, families, old folks, and, more than anything else, lone men, some of them still just boys. She closed the door and looked for a space in another room, but found them all equally overcrowded.

She asked for the bathroom. There were just two per floor, one for women and one for men. She went into the women's to take the shower she'd been needing the whole long road from the Big Chilango. She'd barely been able to take birdbaths at the gas stations. She'd scrubbed her armpits, neck, and face, taken off her pants to shake them out. Once she was almost left behind because she took so long drying herself at the hand dryer. Now she could finally wash all over, and didn't mind that there was no hot water in the hotel shower; it was the same in her hometown. As she was soaping herself she heard someone else come into the bathroom, heard the same someone take two steps and stop, heard them deliberating and heard their hands dip into Makina's rucksack and rootle through her things. She poked her head out. It was a woman in her second youth; she looked tired. She had Makina's lipstick in one hand and started to apply it and didn't stop despite the fact that Makina was watching her and the woman could see she was. She watched her gussy up. She did it slowly and confidently, slid the stick from one side to the other of each lip and then swooped it up as if she'd come to the edge of a cliff, smacked her lips together to even out the color, puckered them for an air kiss. When she was done, still staring into the mirror, the woman said Me? I tell you, I'm gonna start off on the right foot; don't know if makeup will help but at least no one can say I showed up scruffy, you know? And only then did she turn to look at Makina. You look very pretty, Makina said. It'll all go great, you'll see. The woman smiled, said Thanks, hon, put the lipstick back and versed.

After her shower she went back to wandering the rooms where those in flight sweated out the night. Many were sleeplessly waiting for their contact to show and tell them it was time. She deciphered a letter for a very old man who couldn't read, in which his son explained how to find him once he'd crossed. She taught a boy how to say Soap in anglo and explained to another that, as far as she'd been told, you weren't allowed to cook on the sidewalk over there. There were traders, too, who'd just crossed back the other way and slept with their arms around bundles of clothes or toys they'd brought to sell.

She versed to the street. Small groups walked the length of the line, moving farther from the glimmer of the northern city till they found their point of departure. Among them she saw the two boys from the bus negotiating the price of crossing with a couple of men. The men retreated a moment to consult together, talking anglo so the others wouldn't understand. Should we just take 'em? asked the first, and the other said Let 'em wait, too bad if they're in a hurry, Plus, word is that security is tight, For real? For real, Damn, then we really should take 'em, or act like we are: got another little group'll pay us more if we cross 'em right now, Let's put these scrubs out as bait and get the others over, Just what I was thinking. That's what they said, in anglo tongue, and Makina heard it as she sidled up and past them. She kept on going and when she got to where the boys were said Watch it, without turning toward them. The one who had touched her flinched, but the other seemed to realize that Makina was talking about something else, not about what a badass she was. Watch it, they're out to screw you; I was you I'd find someone else, she said and kept on. The youngsters looked at the men, the men guessed Makina had said something, both parties swiftly saw the deal was off, and the men went to find new clients.

She walked up and down along the riverbank until the night waned; then she sat at the water's edge to scan the horizon as she ate one last hunk of brittle, sweet and thick with peanut salt, and just as the sun began to rise she saw a light flicker meaningfully on the other side. Against the clear dawn glow she made out a man and saw that she was the one he was signaling to, so she raised an arm and waved it from side to side. The man switched off his light and went to get something from a truck parked a few feet away. He came back with an enormous inner tube, like from a tractor, tossed it into the water, climbed inside and began to cross the river, propelling himself forward with a tiny oar he'd brought along. As he made his way across, Makina could begin to distinguish the features of the silhouetted man: his skin had the dark polish of long hours spent in the sun, a short salt-and-pepper beard softened his face, in the center of which a large nose, slightly hooked, jutted out; he wore a white shirt darkened by the water scaling his torso, and he carried his own rucksack. Though he gave the impression of being short, as soon as he emerged from the river she saw that he was at least two hands taller than her. And wiry. Every muscle in his arms and neck seemed trained for something specific, something strenuous.

Hey there, he said as soon as he was out of the water. So you're going over for a lil land, I hear.

Ha, said Makina, land's the one thing we got enough of. I'm going for my bro, he's the stupid sap who went over for a little land.

Chucho, said the man, holding out a hand.

Makina, she reciprocated. The man's skin was weather-beaten but pleasing to the touch, warm even though he'd only just versed from the water.

Chucho took a pack of cigarettes from his bag, lit two and gave one to Makina. She inhaled deeply, held the smoke in her lungs—in her head she could see it spiraling gaily—and exhaled.

How'd you recognize me? she asked.

They sent me a picture, full body shot.

For a moment Makina thought he'd make some comment about her looks: You're even cuter in the flesh, or What a tasty surprise, or A sight for sore eyes, or any of that oafishness that makes men feel they're being original, but Chucho just kept smoking, face to the dawn.

Wouldn't it be better to wait till it's dark again? she said. Wouldn't it be too easy for them to spot us now?

Nah, they're tied up somewhere else, he said, winked at her and added I got my contacts.

They finished their smokes and then he said Alright, we're off. He pulled another small oar from his pack and handed it to Makina, pushed the tube back in the water and helped Makina get in in front of him.

The first few feet were easy. Makina could still touch bottom and felt his legs tangle with hers as they advanced; she even, before things got rough, felt him lean in close and sniff her hair, and she was glad she'd had the chance to shower. But suddenly the riverbed ducked away and an icy current began to push their feet away like a living thing, relentless. Row, Chucho said; Makina already was but the tube was being tugged into the current as though adrift. Row, repeated Chucho, this is going to be a bitch. Hardly had he spoken when a torrent of water bounced them out, flipping the tube. Suddenly the world turned cold and green and filled with invisible water monsters dragging her away from the rubber raft; she tried to swim, kicking at whatever was holding her but couldn't figure out which side was up or where Chucho had gone. She didn't know how long she struggled frantically, and then the panic subsided, and she intuited that it made no difference which way she headed or how fast she went, that in the end she'd wind up where she needed to be. She smiled. She felt herself smile. That was when the sound of breaking water replaced the green silence. Chucho dragged her out by the pants with both hands: they'd reached the opposite bank and the inner tube was swirling away in the current as if it had urgent business to attend to.

They lay on the shore, spent and panting. It had hardly been more than a few dozen yards, but on staring up at the sky Makina thought that it was already different, more distant or less blue. Chucho stood, scanned the city at their backs and said Well, now, next part's easier.

3

THE PLACE WHERE THE HILLS MEET

that thing of myths to be on your way, the journey.

First there was nothing. Nothing but a frayed strip of cement over the white earth. Then she made out two mountains colliding in the back of beyond: like they'd come from who knows where and were headed to anyone's guess but had come together at that intense point in the nothingness and insisted on crashing noisily against each other, though the oblivious might think they simply stood there in silence. Yond them hills is the pickup, take you on your way, said Chucho, but we'll make a stop first so you can change.

Then off in the distance she glimpsed a tree and beneath the tree a pregnant woman. She saw her belly before her legs or her face or her hair and saw she was resting there in the shade of the tree. And she thought, if that was any sort of omen it was a good one: a country where a woman with child walking through the desert just lies right down to let her baby grow, unconcerned about anything else. But as they approached she discerned the features of this person, who was no woman, nor was that belly full with child: it was some poor wretch swollen with putrefaction, his eyes and tongue pecked out by buzzards. Makina turned to look at Chucho and see if he too had been fooled, but he hadn't. Chucho told her about how one time he was taking a man back the other way because his wife was dying and they'd gotten lost—this was when he'd only just started crossing folks—and some sonofabitch rancher thought they were headed this direction and it was only because he chased them that they found the way back, but by then it was too late. Cat made it home, Chucho said, but by the time he got there she was already six feet under.

One of the first to strike it rich after going north came back to the Village all full of himself, all la-di-da, all fancy clothes and watches and new words he'd be able to say into his new phone. He made sure to round up every wide-eyed hick he could find, brought each and every one to the switchboard where he planned to teach Makina a lesson in public, as if one time she'd fucked him over, though he claimed he just wanted to show her because she knew about this stuff. He took out two cellphones and gave one to his mother, Here, jefecita, just press this button when you hear the briiiiiiiing and you'll see, just step right outside, and he brandished the other one. He gave Makina two patronizing pats on the forearm and said Tough luck, kid, it had to happen: you're going to be out of a job. Watch and learn. The young man pushed a little key and waited for the zzzz of the dial tone, but the zzzz didn't come. Never mind, no sweat, he said. These new ones don't do that. And proceeded to dial the number of the cellphone his mother was holding to her ear on the other side of the wall. Now at least you could hear peep-peep-peep as he pressed each key, and the wide-eyed stood like ninnies waiting for the thing that they were expecting to happen and yet wishing that it would turn out to be, well, more spectacular somehow, more weird. But the peep-peeps were followed only by silence, a silence

113

that was especially weighty because it seemed as if everyone was holding their breath so as not to spoil the wondrous trick. And the mother was still standing outside, in truth far less concerned about whatever it was her son was up to than about the pot she'd left on the stove, and though the phone was still clamped to her ear she was in fact already telling a neighbor Be an angel, would you? Go check on my stew. And on it went till the guy was left just looking at his phone with all his might, as though enough staring might somehow fix it. Makina held off a bit then said Maybe you should have bought a few cell towers, too? The poor guy turned red when the penny dropped and suddenly he was the only wide-eyed one in the place. That was what Makina said but then she felt mean for messing with him so she gave him a kiss on the cheek and said Don't worry, kid, they'll get here one day.

Before they reached the shack where she was to change clothes, what happened was:

that another truck pulled right up beside them on the road to the mountains; it was black with four searchlights mounted on the roof and the driver was an anglo with dark glasses and a hat with a silver buckle. His eyes shot bullets through the two windows between them, still stepping on it, still stuck to them like glue;

and that Chucho grabbed a cell and started to dial a number but didn't finish till they'd reached the shack, in the foothills, and then dialed the rest when he got out and as soon as they picked up said, in anglo tongue, Hey officer, I got the info I promised, yeah, yeah, right where I said last time, yeah, but be careful, he's armed to the eyeballs, and hung up.

114

The anglo had pulled up ahead and parked a few yards from the shack. He stood by his truck, fingering the grip of a handgun tucked into his waistband. As soon as they went inside Chucho said Gotta be quick, no telling what we're in for now, best leave behind anything might weigh you down. In the shack all there was was a cot and a stove, and on the cot a pair of pants, a t-shirt with an anglo print, and a denim jacket; on the stove, a pot of scalded water. Makina began to undress with her back to Chucho, who stood smoking and staring out the window at the goon on guard outside, and thought how strange it was not to feel scared or angry at having to strip naked with no wall to separate them. She took off her blouse. She could have put on the t-shirt before taking off her pants but she didn't. She took off her pants. She took off her bra and panties, too, though Chucho hadn't told her to, and stood there, looking down at the clothes spread out on the cot, with something almost like an urge to pee and something almost like a bated breath tingling up and down her body. Quick, Chucho insisted; Makina knew he was still staring out the window but his voice enveloped her. She felt that moment of tension without fear go on and on, and then was surprised how much time had passed without her feeling guilty for wanting what she wanted. More than leaving her boyfriend behind she was casting off her guilt the way you might shed belongings. But even those interminable seconds came to an end. She said ok, got dressed. Chucho turned around.

What did you say to that person on the phone? she asked.

Just what I reckon, he said, jerking his head toward outside. Like not only is our rancher here a patriot but he's got his own lil undercover business, like it's not so much he's bothered bout us not having papers as he is bout us muscling in on his act.

You sure?

Chucho shrugged. Maybe the dumbfuck is just in up to his neck.

They stood there a moment, Makina staring at him, Chucho absorbed in his thoughts, one eye on the window the whole time. Then he said Well, whatever's going down, time for it to go down, so if the shit hits the fan you head for that mountain pass and stay on the trail, keep the sun on your back.

She waited for him to start for the door before she took from her rucksack a plastic bag with the note Cora had given her and the package Mr. Aitch had entrusted to her and slipped them into her jacket, and then she went after him. Soon as they versed the rancher approached, revolver in hand, though not pointing it at them.

You just took your last trip, coyote.

I'm no coyote, Chucho said.

Ha! I seen you crossing folks, the man said. And looks like now I caught you in the act.

Not the act I'm denying, said Chucho, tho I'm no coyote.

The anglo's expression indicated that he was engaged in a mighty struggle with the nuances of the concept. He scanned Chucho's face for a few seconds, waiting for clarification. And now, yessir, chose to point the gun at them.

What I'm denying, Chucho went on, Is that you caught us.

Then they all registered the fact they had company. Two police trucks were haring across the open country, top speed but no flashing lights. The minute the rancher was distracted by turning to look, Chucho pounced and grabbed the arm that was holding the gun. The rancher shot to kill but it was a waste of bullets since Chucho had wrestled the muzzle away from the two spots where there were bodies. The rancher was big and strong but all his strength was not enough to regain his balance. In the end Chucho stuck one foot between his two and they both fell to the sand. The police trucks had stopped a dozen yards away and the cops inside took aim from behind the open doors.

Git! said Chucho. Makina moved toward him because even though she knew he was talking to her she thought he was asking her for help. He must be asking for help. Makina wasn't used to having people say Run away.

One more bullet exploded from the revolver; Makina saw the barrel head-on, saw the way it dilated the split second it spat fire and the way it contracted just as the bullet clipped her side. The impact caused her to whirl but not fall, and as she span she took two steps forward and dealt the rancher a kick in the jaw. He was still moving but had lost his sense of direction: he was aiming, like his bullets, for Chucho's neck but where he clawed, all there was was air. Chucho punched him in the chin, which didn't knock the man out but did curb his momentum, and said, stressing each word, I can take care of this. Makina looked to the trucks, then again to the men on the sand, then to the mountains, colliding endlessly before her, and started to run, guns and evil bastards on both sides. She heard them behind her, ordering Freeze, on the ground, but didn't turn, not even when she heard another shot that must have come from a police gun because it sounded different, less powerful than the rancher's.

117

She ran uphill till she could no longer hear shouting behind her, then she turned to look. The cops had the two men in their sights, Chucho's hands on the back of his head and the rancher seemingly unconscious. Another cop looked in Makina's direction but showed no sign of following. Only then did Makina inspect her side. The bullet had entered and versed between two ribs, ignoring her lung, as if it had simply skimmed beneath the surface of her skin so as not to get stuck in her body. She could see the gash of the bullet's path, but it didn't hurt and barely bled. She looked once more to where the men were arguing. Now there was no cop watching her. Chucho was on the ground talking; they stood listening in a semicircle around him. The rancher was still face down.

Makina remembered Chucho's mouth saying I can take care of this. She guessed that he was talking, more than anything, about her, and decided to keep on climbing.

Rucksacks. What do people whose life stops here take with them? Makina could see their rucksacks crammed with time. Amulets, letters, sometimes a *huapango* violin, sometimes a *jaranera* harp. Jackets. People who left took jackets because they'd been told that if there was one thing they could be sure of over there, it was the freezing cold, even if it was desert all the way. They hid what little money they had in their underwear and stuck a knife in their back pocket. Photos, photos, photos. They carried photos like promises but by the time they came back they were in tatters.

In hers, as soon as she'd agreed to go get the kid for Cora, she packed:

118

a small blue metal flashlight, for the darkness she might encounter,

one white blouse and one with colorful embroidery, in case she came across any parties,

three pairs of panties so she'd always have a clean one even if it took a while to find a washhouse,

a latin–anglo dictionary (those things were by old men and for old men, outdated the second they left the press, true, but they still helped, like people who don't really know where a street is and yet point you in the right direction),

a picture her little sister had drawn in fat, round strokes that featured herself, Makina and Cora in ascending order, left to right and short to tall,

a bar of *xithé* soap,

a lipstick that was more long-lasting than it was dark and, as provisions: amaranth cakes and peanut brittle.

She was coming right back, that's why that was all she took.

4

THE OBSIDIAN MOUND

When she reached the top of the saddle between the two mountains it began to snow. Makina had never seen snow before and the first thing that struck her as she stopped to watch the weightless crystals raining down was that something was burning. One came to perch on her eyelashes; it looked like a stack of crosses or the map of a palace, a solid and intricate marvel at any rate, and when it dissolved a few seconds later she wondered how it was that some things in the world—some countries, some people—could seem eternal when everything was actually like that miniature ice palace: one-of-a-kind, precious, fragile. She felt a sudden stab of disappointment but also a slight subsiding of the fear that had been building since she'd versed from home.

On the other side of the mountains was the truck Chucho had told her about. She went up to it, opened the passenger door and said Are you Aitch's man? The driver jumped out of his skin then tried to recover his hard-boiled slouch, upped his nose as if to say S'right, and finally jerked his head to signal Get in.

On the way the driver turned to look at her every little while, as though hoping she'd try to talk to him so he could refuse, but Makina had no interest in the challenge; she should have been exhausted but what she felt was an over-whelming impatience. She turned to the window to look out without seeing. If she didn't get back soon, what would become of all those people who had no way of communicating with their kith and kin? She had to get back, because Cora was counting on her; and what about the switchboard, how would it look and feel without her? Ay, the guilt, reducing reality to a clenched fist with set hours.

The city was an edgy arrangement of cement particles and yellow paint. Signs prohibiting things thronged the streets, leading citizens to see themselves as ever protected, safe, friendly, innocent, proud, and intermittently bewildered, blithe, and buoyant; salt of the only earth worth knowing. They flourished in supermarkets, cornucopias where you could have more than everyone else or something different or a newer brand or a loaf of bread a little bigger than every-one else's. Makina just dented cans and sniffed bottles and thought it best to verse, and it was when she saw the anglo-gaggle at the self-checkouts that she noticed how miserable they looked in front of those little digital screens, and the way they nearly-nearly jumped every time the machine went bleep! at each item. And how on versing out to the street they sought to make amends for their momentary one-up by becoming wooden again so as not to offend anyone.

Out on the concrete and steel-girder plain, though, she sensed another presence straight off, scattered about like bolts fallen from a window: on street corners, on scaffolding, on sidewalks; fleeting looks of recognition quickly concealed and then evasive. These were her compatriots, her homegrown, armed with work: builders, florists, loaders, drivers; playing it sly so as not to let on to any shared objective, and instead just, just, just: just there to take orders. They were the same as back home but with less whistling, and no begging.

She was seduced by something less clear-cut as she wandered by the restaurants: unfamiliar sweetness and spiciness, concoctions that had never before passed her lips or her nose, rapturous fried feasts. Places serving food that was strange but with something familiar mixed in, something recognizable in the way the dishes were finished off. So she visited the restaurants, too, with the brevity imposed by glaring managers who guessed She's not here to eat, and it wasn't until the fourth restaurant that she realized they were here, too, more armed than anyplace else, cooks and helpers and dishwashers, ruling the food at the farthest outposts.

All cooking is Mexican cooking, she said to herself. And then she said Ha. It wasn't true, but she liked saying it just the same.

The driver jerked up his palms when he saw Makina take out the package from Mr. Aitch. You don't give nothing to me. Didn't you know that? He dropped her on a deserted street and said Here's where they'll tell you where to take it. Since there was nobody around she ambled through a supermarket and sniffed restaurants. When she returned, a flower store had opened; an old man was sitting at the entrance, resting one hand on a cane and bringing a piece of bread to his mouth with the other. Makina planted herself in front of him. They looked at each other. Again Makina made as if to take the packet out but the old man said Wait, go clean up first and then I'll take you. With his cane he pointed to a little door at the back of the store. Makina went through it, washed her hands and face; the wound on her ribs was dry and when she rubbed the soap across it hardly even stung. When she versed from the bathroom the old man was standing up. Come with me, he said. See those men? Makina saw two guys in a black ride with silver rims. Cops, wondering who you are, he went on. We're going to walk till they get sidetracked. They began walking. The car followed close behind, suddenly accelerated and disappeared, but soon returned to follow them at a distance.

I'm taking you to the stadium, the old man said. If they stop trailing us, you hand it over there; meantime I'll tell you about your kin.

Makina was overcome by foreboding. Is he dead?

No, no, alive and kicking like a mule, he's fine; you'll find him changed, but still, he got here ok. Like you, he brought a little something from Mr. Aitch and things got rough, but then he went off on his business.

Do you know where?

The old man said Help me walk. Makina took his arm and the old man smoothly slipped her a piece of paper with his other hand. Address's right here.

They kept walking. The black car slowed beside them, the occupants eyeballed for a few seconds and took off.

Think it's safe? Makina asked.

Don't know, but it's got to be done.

The stadium loomed before them. So, what do they use that for?

They play, said the old man. Every week the anglos play a

game to celebrate who they are. He stopped, raised his cane and fanned the air. One of them whacks it, then sets off like it was a trip around the world, to every one of the bases out there, you know the anglos have bases all over the world, right? Well the one who whacked it runs from one to the next while the others keep taking swings to distract their enemies, and if he doesn't get caught he makes it home and his people welcome him with open arms and cheering.

Do you like it?

Tsk, me, I'm just passing through.

How long you been here?

Going on fifty years . . . Here we are.

They were standing at one of the doors to the stadium. The old man gave a whistle, the door opened, the old man said Get it over with, and turned away.

The darkest kid Makina had ever seen in her life pointed to a corridor. She walked down it toward the light. At the end she was instantly overcome by the sight of a vast expanse, two rival visions of beauty: the bottom an immense green diamond rippling in its own reflection; and above, embracing it, tens of thousands of folded black chairs, an obsidian mound barbed with flint, sharp and glimmering.

She was standing there, dazzled, when from other tunnels around her more men emerged, ten or fifteen or thirty all at once, all black but some blacker than others, some sinewy as if they'd grown up in mountain air, others puffy like aquatic animals, many bald but a few with long matted hair down to their waists. All looking at her and walking toward her, calm and cool but with faces that clearly conveyed they were serious motherfuckers.

Don't let my associates scare you, she suddenly heard behind her, in latin tongue. They're not such tough sonsof-bitches, just had to learn to look like it.

Down the corridor she'd walked, a man limped nearer, his features becoming clearer as he was gradually bathed in light: his blazing blond hair was streaked with orange highlights, he held a cigar in one hand and wore mirrored shades. Makina had never laid eyes on him before but there was no mistaking who he was. Mr. P, the fourth top dog, had fled the Little Town after a turf war with Mr. Aitch and every once in a while you'd hear how one way or another they were goading each other from afar. What had Makina gotten herself into? Did Mr. P think he could mess with Mr. Aitch by messing with her?

You got nothing to fear from me neither, girl, said Mr. P, suspecting her guts were churning. And not because Aitch and I have made peace. We do business, sure, but who says that's not just another way to eat the dish cold?

Makina noticed that from his belt hung a long, thin knife and that Mr. P patted it nonstop. Very slowly, she at last pulled out the packet that was for him. Mr. P held out his hand, weighed up the package without taking his eyes off her, and passed it to one of his associates. He patted and patted his knife and smiled at Makina while the associates opened the package, closed the package and in anglo said We're cool. Mr. P, though, kept leering and smiling at Makina and patting his dangling knife, and she wanted to go now but couldn't muster enough of a voice for even the first syllable.

Wouldn't you like to come work for me, child? asked Mr. P, eyeing her crotch.

I'm here for my brother.

Of course, the brother.

Mr. P stopped looking, scratched his chin and repeated The brother, the brother.

His eyes scanned the stadium with idle curiosity, he turned, and the associates began to verse leisurely down the tunnels, until Makina was all alone.

5

THE PLACE WHERE THE WIND
CUTS LIKE A KNIFE

They are homegrown and they are anglo and both things with rabid intensity; with restrained fervor they can be the meekest and at the same time the most querulous of citizens, albeit grumbling under their breath. Their gestures and tastes reveal both ancient memory and the wonderment of a new people. And then they speak. They speak an intermediary tongue that Makina instantly warms to because it's like her: malleable, erasable, permeable; a hinge pivoting between two like but distant souls, and then two more, and then two more, never exactly the same ones; something that serves as a link.

More than the midpoint between homegrown and anglo their tongue is a nebulous territory between what is dying out and what is not yet born. But not a hecatomb. Makina senses in their tongue not a sudden absence but a shrewd metamorphosis, a self-defensive shift. They might be talking in perfect latin tongue and without warning begin to talk in perfect anglo tongue and keep it up like that, alternating between a thing that believes itself to be perfect and a thing that believes itself to be perfect, morphing back and forth between two beasts until out of carelessness or clear intent they suddenly stop switching tongues and start speaking that other one. In it brims nostalgia for the land they left or never knew when they use the words with which they name objects; while actions are alluded to with an anglo verb conjugated latin-style, pinning on a sonorous tail from back there.

Using in one tongue the word for a thing in the other makes the attributes of both resound: if you say Give me fire when they say Give me a light, what is not to be learned about fire, light and the act of giving? It's not another way of saying things: these are new things. The world happening anew, Makina realizes: promising other things, signifying other things, producing different objects. Who knows if they'll last, who knows if these names will be adopted by all, she thinks, but there they are, doing their damnedest.

The paper the old man had slipped her bore an address in another city but it seemed there was no need to verse this one to get to that one: it was simply a matter of riding busses and crossing streets and passing malls and after lots of the first and even more of the second and several of the third, she'd arrive.

She almost didn't realize when she reached it, because the cities had no center for avenues to radiate from. She just suddenly started seeing the name of the other place on stores and fire trucks. She kept walking the way she'd been told by some homegrown anglos she'd spoken to, and as she made her way the sky got redder and the air began to ice up.

Her lips were split and her palms cracked if she pulled them from her jacket pockets.

Eight times she asked before she found the spot and every time the abject answer turned out to be some bleak tundra where they sent her to another bleak tundra:

She asked the way to the city and they told her Over there (finger pointing to where the sun comes up).

She asked farther on for the way to the suburb and they told her There's four with that name, but maybe she wanted the one by the bridge.

She asked farther on for the way to the bridge, but they told her she didn't want that suburb but the one with the zoo.

She asked farther on for the way to the zoo and they told her it was near the statue of a man in a frock coat.

She asked farther on for the way to the statue of the man in a frock coat and they said Can't you see, it's right behind you.

Then she asked for the way to the street written down and they said This is it.

She asked for the way to her brother, perhaps too urgently, and they shrugged.

She asked finally for the way to the promised land and that person looked annoyed before responding.

There was still some light in the sky but it was turning dark, like a giant pool of drying blood.

Her brother had sent two or three messages back with assorted migrants on their way home. Two or three and not two, or three; Makina couldn't say for sure because after the first one the one that followed and maybe one more were the same old story.

The first one said:

I haven't found the land yet, but it won't be long now, you'll see.

Everything's so stiff here, it's all numbered and people look you in the eye but they don't say anything when they do.

They celebrate here, too, but they don't dance or pray, it's not in honor of anyone. The only real big celebration is the turkey feast, which is a good one because all you do is eat and eat.

It's really lonely here, but there's lots of stuff. I'm going to bring you some when I come. I just have to take care of this and then I'll be back, you'll see.

The second one didn't mention the country or the land or his plans. It said:

I'm fine, I have a job now.

And the third, if it existed, might've made the same claim, this way:

I said I was fine so stop asking.

It had taken everything she had just to pronounce the eight tundras. To cleave her way through the cold on her own, sustained by nothing but an ember inside; to go from one street to another without seeing a difference; to encounter barricades that held people back for the benefit of cars. Or to encounter people who spoke none of the tongues she knew: whole barrios of clans from other frontiers, who questioned her with words that seemed traced in the air. The weariness she felt at the monuments of another history. The disdain, the suspicious looks. And again the cold, getting colder, burrowing into her with insolence.

And when she arrived and saw what she'd come to find it was sheer emptiness.

And yet machines were still at work. That was the first thing she noticed when they pointed the place out to her: excavators obstinately scratching the soil as if they needed urgently to empty the earth; but the breadth of that abyss and the clean cut of its walls didn't correspond to the modest exertion of the machines. Whatever once was there had been pulled out by the roots, expelled from this world; it no longer existed.

I don't know what they told you, declared the irritated anglo, I don't know what you think you lost but you ain't going to find it here, there was nothing here to begin with.

6

THE PLACE WHERE FLAGS WAVE

Scum, she heard as she climbed the eighth hill from which, she was sure, she'd catch sight of her brother. You lookin to get what you deserve, you scum? She opened her eyes. A huge redheaded anglo who stank of tobacco was staring at her. Makina knew the bastard was just itching to kick her or fuck her and got slowly to her feet without taking her eyes off him, because when you turn your back in fear is when you're at the greatest risk of getting your ass kicked; she opened the door and versed.

She'd been asking after her brother around the edges of the abyss. She'd approach anybody she heard speaking latin tongue, give a verbal portrait of her brother, imitate his singsong accent, mention his favorite colors, repeat the story of the land he was there to claim, state his place of birth, list all the things he could do, beg them, please, to try to remember if they'd ever come across him. Until the frigid squall forced her to duck into an ATM booth, where she curled up like a dog and after much bone-trembling managed to fall asleep and dreamed that she was scaling one, two, three, seven hills, and when she made it to the top of the eighth she was awakened by the thunderous contempt of the redhead.

It hadn't fully dawned yet—the sky was barely a reddish exhalation that hadn't quite made up its mind to spread over the earth—but by this time the people who might have information for her were already back in the hustle and bustle. She began to walk, rubbing her palms red and pricking up her ears. As she passed the back alley of a restaurant she heard not only a familiar lilt but a voice she knew. She peeked in and saw the youngster from the bus dragging metal cans up beside the restaurant door; he was working energetically, whistling a song from another time, and though he wore only pants and a t-shirt he didn't seem to mind the early-morning chill. He had a small bandage on the hand that Makina had schooled. He smiled on seeing her and made his way over, but as he got closer his face clouded, more with sadness than with fear. I must look terrible, she thought.

Fell on your feet, huh? said Makina.

Damn straight, the boy responded. How bout you?

Ok, but I'm not there yet; there's still someone I have to find.

Your kin came for a grind, too?

Yeah, but I don't know where.

The kid pondered for a moment and then said Come with me.

They walked into the restaurant. Makina followed him past rows of cauldrons boiling on the stove, knives, hatchets, cressets, skillets, brokeneck chickens and flopping fish, to a corner where there was a woman deveining a pile of red peppers. She was pale and thin and had an extremely sweet face, but to Makina she looked like Cora, perhaps because of the way she worked, as if undressing her grandchildren for the

133

shower, or because straight away, like with Cora, she felt she could trust her. The woman raised her eyes, fixed them for a second on Makina without ceasing her work on the chiles, and lowered them once more.

Doña, I'm bringing you this girl here, the youngster said. She's looking for one of her kin, and since you seen so many folks come through . . .

Yes, I know, the woman said, but made no attempt to fill the silence that followed.

What? asked Makina. What do you know, señora?

I know who you are.

Did you ever meet my brother?

The woman nodded.

Turned up all sickly and scared as a stray dog, she said. We gave him soup and a sweater and let him sleep under the dish cabinet. Bout a year ago it was, maybe less. Round about that time an anglo woman came, seemed so sad, asking if we didn't have a young man, said she needed one urgent for a job, she seemed like a good person and just so sad, and I told your kin he should go see if that would work for him, cause like I say she looked like a good person but real real mournful and I had no way to know what it was she needed. Your brother went to see her and never came back. Reckon it worked out for him.

And do you know where he went?

Let the boy here take you; I showed him the barrio.

The woman gave the youngster an address and Makina was already rushing him out to the street when she stopped and looked back to ask How did you know who I was? Did my brother tell you how to recognize me?

That too, yes. Told me he had a sister who just by looking at her you could tell she was smart and schooled, said the woman. Yes, that too.

After half a block the youngster was already lagging and decided to give Makina the address of the house where her brother had gone. Makina flew; she literally felt her feet not touching the ground, as if she could float, scissoring her legs till she found her brother and brought him home without setting foot on foreign soil again.

The house was beautiful and big and pink and a wooden fence surrounded it. Makina opened the little gate in the middle of the fence, went up to the front door, rang the bell, waited. She heard a man's footsteps approach and got her hopes up that it was him, that he himself would be the one to open the door, that they'd be reunited right then, no more delays. The door opened and there stood a small man with glasses, wrapped in a purple bathrobe. He was black. Never in her life had she seen so many black people up close, and all of a sudden they seemed to be the key to her quest. Makina glared as though reproaching him for being skinnier and blacker and older than her brother, as though this man were attempting to pass for the other. She was about to say something when he beat her to it with I could put on a blond wig if you like.

Makina was thrown for a second and then laughed, embarrassed.

Sorry, she said in anglo, it's just that I was expecting someone else to open the door.

Someone white? Do you think this is a white person's house?

No, no . . .

Well, right you are, this is a white person's house, there's not a thing I can do about it, except dress like a white person. Do you like my robe?

No . . . Yes . . . I mean, it's just I was expecting someone different.

A different black man? Are you saying I'm not black enough?

Makina laughed. The man laughed. Suddenly her anxiety had passed. For the first time since she'd crossed she felt welcome, even if she still wasn't invited in.

No, not white or black, I'm looking for my brother. They told me he came here to work, in this house.

Oh shoot, the man said with exaggerated disappointment, I knew my prayers couldn't have been answered with such celerity . . . Last night I knelt down and begged the Lord: Lord, send me a woman to relieve me of my misery.

I'm sorry . . .

Right, I know, the brother. He's not here. I'm here. The family that lived here moved. To another continent. They sold the house and I bought it. I don't know why they left, but times are changing and this is a lovely place to stay put.

Makina felt all of the strength she'd been recovering from her own ashes begin to ebb, felt herself extinguishing, felt she wouldn't be able to verse from this one last dead end and that her luck had finally run out. To hell with it all, she thought, to hell with this guy and that one, to hell with all this shit, I'm going to hang myself from a lamppost and let the wind whip me around like an old rag; I'm going to start crying and then I'm going to go to hell too. She gestured farewell to the black man and prepared to go.

There's one left, though, he said.

Makina stared intently, as if trying to read his lips.

What?

They left the oldest son behind. He's a soldier. If you go to the army base you'll find him there.

Makina had no idea what so-called respectable people were referring to when they talked about Family. She'd known families that were truncated, extended, bitter, friendly, guileful, doleful, hospitable, ambitious, but never had she known a Happy Family of the sort people talked about, the sort so many swore to defend; all of them were more than just one thing, or they were all the same thing but in completely different ways: none were only fun-loving or solely stingy, and the stories that made any two laugh had nothing in common.

She'd seen people who'd run off to save their families and others who'd run off to be saved from them. Families full of endless table chat as easygoing as families that loved each other without words. (In hers there were just three women right now. Her heart skipped a beat when she thought of her little sister; it only started back up when she concluded that, like her, she'd know how to take care of herself.)

Plus, all families had started off in some mysterious way: to repopulate the earth, or by accident, or by force, or out of boredom; and it's all a mystery what each will become. One time she'd been in the middle of an argument between sweethearts. The woman had run to the switchboard, planted herself behind Makina and stood there responding to each of the man's grievances; it was sheer pigheadedness till Makina began to rephrase their respective complaints: You like my

137

cousin better, you can keep her, She says that was low, you getting with her cousin, What are you bitching about? I'm the same cat I was when you met me, He says he's acting like the man you wanted him to be, Oh, then me too, so don't get in my face cause I already knew that friend of yours, She says what's good for the gander is good for the goose, But you'd never done nothing with him before and me and your cousin was an item, He says that's apples and oranges, I don't care if you was an item back in the day, but I damn sure care if you still are, She says to stop playing dumb, It was just one kiss, the last one, He says they were saying goodbye, Oh, right, then mine was a goodbye, too, She says why can't she if you're still messing around, I'm not saying you can't, but it bugged me when everyone found out, He says he's not that jealous but you shouldn't be so brazen. Then they both shut up and Makina concluded I think you're both saying that the both of you could be more discreet. For a while after that, every time she bumped into them they'd thank her for getting them back together. Then she didn't see them anymore.

On her way to the army base Makina passed a building whose steps were crowded with people holding multicolored flags; her excitement and hurry having subsided, she stopped to see what it was about. There were couples holding hands lining up to see a very solemn man who said something to them and after he said it everyone cried and there was rice and clapping and rejoicing galore. They were getting married. Makina was so dazzled by the beauty of the ceremony that she didn't at first notice that the couples were either men or women but not men and women, and on realizing it she felt

138

moved by how many tears were being shed, like flowers from their eyes, over how hard it had been to get there, and she wished that the people she'd known in the same situation could have been that happy. What she couldn't understand was why the ring, the official, the godparents mattered so. Makina had admired the nerve of her friends who were that way inclined, compared to the tedious smugness of so-called normal marriages; she'd conveyed secret messages, lent her home for the loving that could not speak its name and her clothes for liberation parades. She'd witnessed other ways to love . . . and now they were acting just the same. She felt slightly let down but then said to herself, what did she know. It must be, she thought, that they know other marriages, good ones where people don't split up, where fathers don't leave and they each keep speaking to the other. That must be why they're so happy, and don't mind imitating people who've always despised them. Or perhaps they just want the papers, she said to herself, any kind of papers, even if it's only to fit in; maybe being different gets old after a while.

She went on her way, toward the west, and after many blocks made out another array of flags, equally pretty but all lined up and all the same size. This was where the soldiers were.

7

THE PLACE WHERE
PEOPLE'S HEARTS ARE EATEN

Wait here, the soldier said.

As she waited at the entry booth for the anglo whose name the black man had given her, Makina wondered what she'd do if they brought bad news, if they told her that her brother had died or that they had no clue where he might be. Mr. Aitch might lend a hand in exchange for an additional favor, but that would mean mixing with crooks again just for the sake of a tip-off she couldn't necessarily count on. And what was the point of calling the cops when your measure of good fortune consisted of having them not know you exist.

The soldier returned to the booth and sat down behind his desk. He opened a folder and went back to concentrating on the papers he'd been reading before Makina arrived. He'd only just started when he seemed to remember she was there. He looked up and told her the soldier would be with her right away, and went back to his reading.

A few minutes later the door opened and there appeared before her, dressed in military uniform, her very own brother.

Neither one at first recognized the specter of the other. In fact, Makina stood up, greeted him and began to express her

140

gratitude and ask a question before picking up on the soldier's uncanny resemblance to her brother and the unmistakable way in which they differed; he had the same sloping forehead and stiff hair, but looked hardier, and more washed-out. In that fraction of a second she realized her mistake, and that this was her brother, but also that that didn't undo the mistake. She stopped breathing for a second, placed the fingertips of one hand on the desk so as not to lose her balance, and reached out the other to touch the apparition that was this man she had not asked to see. He took her arm, said to the other soldier I'll be right back and versed out to the street with Makina.

They walked awhile in silence. They turned their heads to look at one another, first him, now her, then stared ahead again, disbelieving. They pondered some more what each should say. Finally, still staring straight ahead, he started off:

Did you have a hard time finding me?

Kind of; I only found you when I stopped trying.

How's Cora?

Alive, said Makina; she thought of the message she'd brought him but instead she said What about the land?

Her brother chuckled. You went to see it, didn't you?

Makina nodded.

After that I bounced from back alley to back alley and ass-kicking to ass-kicking, till I met the old lady at the restaurant. She fed me soup till I had strength enough to come home.

But you didn't come home.

No, he said, I didn't come home.

Her brother told Makina an incredible story. After the land fiasco he was too ashamed to return, which is why he accepted the first job that came his way. That woman had come offering the earth itself for his assistance. She spoke latin tongue and asked for his help with every term of entreaty she could find in the dictionary. She took him to her house, introduced him to her husband, to her young daughter, and, after waiting for him to come out of his room, to a bad-tempered teen.

This is who you're going to help, said the woman. But I wanted you to meet the whole family you'll be saving.

He must have been about the same age as him, just barely grown-up. Like him, without consulting his family he'd decided to do something to prove his worth as a man and had joined the army, and in a few days they were going to send him to the other side of the world to fight against who knew what people that had who knew what horrific ways of killing. He was of age, but acted like a child: for the whole insane hour that their interview went on he kept clenching his fists and pursing his lips and only looked up when everything was settled. Over the following days he approached Makina's brother several times to ask who he was, where he came from, if he was scared; but he didn't speak enough of their tongue to respond and only said the name of his Village or the term for its inhabitants, which didn't begin to explain his previous life, or he simply said no, he wasn't scared. The other adolescent nodded and went off tight-lipped, as if there were something he had to say but didn't dare.

This was the deal: Makina's brother would pass himself off as the other. On his return, the family would pay him a sum of money. A large sum, they specified. Plus, he could keep the kid's papers, his name, and his numbers. If he didn't make it back, they'd send the money to his family. And you, would they send you back, too? Makina asked. We didn't discuss that, he replied.

He accepted without quibbling. He was going off with the most powerful army in the world and he thought that was enough of a guarantee that he'd make it back in one piece. He spent his last days before he shipped out at the family's house. They made him learn by heart the answers he'd have to give when he reported, they taught him to copy the signature of the kid he was replacing, he memorized his social security number, they gave him pancakes and warm milk, he was treated well. All those nights he slept in the boy's room and wondered why anyone would give up such a soft bed, but he answered his own question immediately: everyone had to do something for themselves.

The morning he turned up at the barracks he felt an unspeakable fear from the moment he opened his eyes and remembered that that was the day he was going off to war, but he was aware that there was no turning back and he announced himself and answered the questions they asked and signed with the signature he'd learned. The officers who received him looked doubtful at the discrepancy between his name and his face, between his fear and the fact that he'd volunteered, but they took him all the same. And off he went to war.

What was it like? Makina asked. The war.

Her brother tried to avoid the question with a shrug of his shoulders, but the gesture itself betrayed him: when his shoulders returned to their place it was as if they were dragging his whole body down and his expression hardened from the inside out.

Why do you want to know, he said. You wouldn't understand.

So I can understand you.

He took a breath, suddenly raised a hand and tugged Makina's hair; he lowered it again, rubbed it with his other hand and nodded.

It's not like in the movies, he said. I know that here everything seems like in the movies, but it's not like that there. You spend days and days shut in and it's like nothing's going on at all and then one day you go out but you don't know who you're fighting or where you're going to find them. And suddenly you hear your homie died that morning and no one saw where the bullet came from, or you come across a bomb nobody saw get thrown, but there it was, waiting for you. So you gotta go look for them. But when you find them they're not doing jack and you just gotta believe it was them, they were the ones, otherwise you go nuts.

Did you get hurt? Makina asked.

He shook his head and pooched out his lips, neither proud nor relieved.

Not a scratch, he said. So happened that whenever things kicked off I was taking guys out, not getting took . . . Some get a taste for it right away. Not me. Still, you know: if tears are gonna fall, better their house than mine . . .

After he finished his few months' stint he returned to the family's house. He didn't ask them for anything, just went, knocked on the door and got let in. They stared at him with eyes like saucers, astonished to see him there, alive and decorated: alive. He saw it made them uneasy to have him back, as if he were a stranger who'd shown up to talk about something that bore no relation to their white dishes and their white sheets and their station wagon. The father congratulated him, offered him a beer, thanked him on behalf of his country and then began to stammer something about how hard it was to get the money together and how complicated it would be for Makina's brother to use his son's identity and about the possibility of him working for them instead and that way, if he wanted, he could stay in the country legally. But the mother didn't let him finish. Said No. Said We're going to keep our promise. But everyone here knows him, said the father, referring to his offspring. Then we'll go someplace else, the mother replied. We'll change our name, reinvent ourselves, the mother replied.

Since they'd assumed he wasn't coming back, they didn't have the money they'd promised; they gave him something, less than he was hoping for but much more than he could have earned bussing or waiting tables in that time. And they went away.

They bumped into a soldier who started talking to Makina's brother.

Last night I will go to the bar they will tell us about, he said in anglo.

Oh, yeah? How was it, angloed her brother in return.

There will be many women, they will be so pretty, and they will all like the uniform.

Is that so? You speak to any?

Yes, I will speak, I will speak all night, she will give me her number, I will kiss her a little.

First base, huh? Good for you!

I will get very drunk after that. She will go but she will promise that we will see each other again.

Makina's brother laughed and slapped the guy's back, and he carried on his way to the barracks gate.

What was that about? asked Makina.

He's homegrown, he said. Joined up just like me, but still doesn't speak the lingo. Whereas me, I learned it, so every time we see each other he wants to practice. He speaks all one day in past tense, all one day in present, all one day in future, so he can learn his verbs. Today was the future.

And there he was. It was an incredible story, but there was her brother in his battle-worn uniform, alive and in one piece. All of a sudden he had money and a new name, but no clue what to do, where to go, what the path of the person with that name should be.

There wasn't any land to claim. Course you already know that, he said. So I was left hanging.

He stopped and reflected for a minute.

I guess that's what happens to everybody who comes, he continued. We forget what we came for, but there's this reflex to act like we still have some secret plan.

Why not leave, then?

Not now. Too late. I already fought for these people. There must be something they fight so hard for. So I'm staying in the army while I figure out what it is.

But won't they just send you back over there?

He held up his palms. Who knows, we'll see.

They'd made their way back to the entrance to the barracks. They stood there, in silence, until he said I got to go.

Makina nodded. She didn't know what else to say.

You have enough to get back? he asked, anxious. He pulled out his wallet, took out a few bills and handed them to her. Makina accepted them mechanically.

I got to go, he repeated.

He leaned in toward her, and as he gave her a hug said Give Cora a kiss from me. He said it the same way he gave her the hug, like it wasn't his sister he was hugging, like it wasn't his mother he was sending a kiss to, but just a polite platitude. Like he was ripping out her heart, like he was cleanly extracting it and placing it in a plastic bag and storing it in the fridge to eat later.

Sure, said Makina. I'll tell her.

Her brother looked at her one last time, as if from a long way away, turned and walked into the barracks. Makina stood staring at the entrance for some time. Then she pulled out the envelope that Cora had given her, took out the sheet of paper it contained and read it.

Come on back now, it said in Cora's crooked writing. Come on back now, we don't expect anything from you.

8

THE SNAKE THAT LIES IN WAIT

She'd already left the barracks when she heard You too! Assume the position! You too! She turned and saw a horribly pasty policeman pointing at her. Are you deaf? Get in line.

In a vacant lot pooled with black water were half a dozen men on their knees, staring at the ground. They all were or looked homegrown. Makina took her place beside them.

You think you can just come here and put your feet up without earning it, said the cop. Well I got news for you: patriots like me are on the lookout and we're going to teach you some manners. Lesson one: get used to falling in. You want to come here, fall in and ask permission, you want to go to the doctor, fall in and ask permission, you want to say a fucking word to me, fall in and ask permission. Fall in and ask permission. Civilized, that's the way we do things around here! We don't jump fences and we don't dig tunnels.

Out the corner of her eye Makina could see the cop's tongue poking out as he talked, all pink and pointy. She could see, too, that even though he didn't draw, he also didn't take his hand off the holster where his gun was. Suddenly the cop addressed one of the others, the one beside her.

What you got there?

He took two steps toward him and repeated What you got there?

The man was holding a little book and gripped it tighter when the cop came close. He resisted a bit but finally let him snatch it away.

Ha, said the cop after glancing at it. Poetry. Lookie here at the educated worker, comes with no money, no papers, but hey, poems. You a romantic? A poet? A writer? Looks like we're going to find out.

He ripped out one of the last pages, laid it on the book's cover, pulled a pencil from his shirt and gave it all to the man.

Write.

The man looked up, bewildered.

I told you to write, not look at me, you piece of shit. Keep your eyes on the paper and write why you think you're up the creek, why you think your ass is in the hands of this patriotic officer. Or don't you know what you did wrong? Sure you do. Write.

The man pressed the pencil to the paper and began to trace a letter but his trembling prevented him. He dropped the pencil, picked it up, and tried again. He couldn't compose a single word, just nervous scribble.

Makina suddenly snatched the pencil and book away. The cop roared I didn't tell you to . . . But he fell silent on seeing that Makina had begun to write with determination. He kept a close watch on her progress, smiling and sardonic the whole time, though he was disconcerted and couldn't hide it.

Makina wrote without stopping to think which word was better than which other or how the message was turning out. She wrote ten lines and when she was done she placed the pencil on the book and fixed her gaze upon it. The cop waited a few seconds, then said Give me that, took the sheet of paper and began to read aloud:

We are to blame for this destruction, we who don't speak your tongue and don't know how to keep quiet either. We who didn't come by boat, who dirty up your doorsteps with our dust, who break your barbed wire. We who came to take your jobs, who dream of wiping your shit, who long to work all hours. We who fill your shiny clean streets with the smell of food, who brought you violence you'd never known, who deliver your dope, who deserve to be chained by neck and feet. We who are happy to die for you, what else could we do? We, the ones who are waiting for who knows what. We, the dark, the short, the greasy, the shifty, the fat, the anemic. We the barbarians.

The cop had started off in a mock-portentous voice but gradually abandoned the histrionics as he neared the last line, which he read almost in a whisper. After that he went on staring at the paper as if he'd gotten stuck on the final period. When he finally looked up, his rage, or his interest in his captives, seemed to have dissolved. He crumpled the paper into a ball and tossed it behind him. Then he looked away, turned his back, spoke over the radio to someone and took off.

Makina stood as soon as the cop had gone, but the others took some time to realize they weren't under arrest. They looked at one another, half glad and half mistrustful, then looked at Makina but couldn't say anything to her because she'd started walking again and all they could make out was her silhouette against the sun.

9

THE OBSIDIAN PLACE WITH NO WINDOWS OR HOLES FOR THE SMOKE

She couldn't stop, she had to keep walking even if she didn't know how she was going to get back. It was the rhythm, it was her burden-free body, it was the soft sound of her own panting that pushed her on. She quickened her step; with the ashen sun head-on she walked down gray streets and past houses that were all the same, like little boxes lined up in a storefront window.

She came to a park all atwitter with birds about to go to sleep. She walked straight through the middle of it, not around it on the sidewalk, and with each step her feet—pad, pad, pad—left an imprint on the earth. The evening clouded over until you couldn't see more than one step ahead, and yet Makina didn't stop: she walked quickly—pad, pad, pad—guiding herself by the trilling in the trees. Suddenly she heard Watch how you go, darlin.

She turned to see who had spoken, because they'd said it in latin tongue, and saw that there, sitting on a bench looking exactly like himself and also quite different—like varnished over, like meaner, or with a bigger nose—was Chucho, grinning at her. First she saw the ember, then the man who made it glow. Makina felt herself smile though she didn't feel the emotion behind the smile because she'd somehow been emptied of feelings by now.

What are you doing here? she asked.

Doing my thing, looking out for you.

Don't you work for Aitch? Mr. Q is the one who was supposed to help me on this side.

I work for whoever hires me. Never stopped watching you, I know where you been and how tough things got.

Things are tough all over, but here I'm all mixed up, I just don't understand this place.

Don't let it get you down. They don't understand it either, they live in fear of the lights going out, as if every day wasn't already made of lightning and blackouts. They need us. They want to live forever but still can't see that for that to work they need to change color and number. But it's already happening.

Chucho took a drag on his cigarette so deep he almost consumed it all. Then he said And now you're here, follow me. He stood and Makina walked beside him. They left the park, entered a little maze of streets that looked like they belonged to some other city and stopped before a low, narrow door behind which nothing could be seen.

Go on in, Chucho said, pointing.

Here? What is this place?

Here's where they'll give you a hand.

Makina crouched down to fit through the door, and on taking the first step felt a cold wind coming from inside but didn't get cold herself; she saw the top of a spiral staircase. She began to descend, turned to see if Chucho was following but he had stayed at the door, blew her a kiss, moved out of the frame and Makina caught a glimpse of the last rays of sun. Then she went on down. After four spiral turns she came to another door, which was answered by a handsome old woman with very long white fingernails and a powdered face, wearing a butterfly pin that held back the folds of her dress. Over the door was a sign that said *Verse*. She tried to remember how to say verse in any of her tongues but couldn't. This was the only word that came to her lips. Verse. The woman drew two cigarettes from a black case, lit them both and held one out. Makina took it and stepped through.

The place was like a sleepwalker's bedroom: specific yet inexact, somehow unreal and yet vivid; there were lots of people, very calm, all smoking, and though she saw no ventilation shafts nor felt any currents the air didn't smell. Like a song from long ago, a sudden apprehension made her think something terrible was going to occur any second. Something's about to happen, something's about to happen. She tensed and felt she loved her skin, but the tension soon gave way, lulled by the only clear and distinguishable sound in the place. She hadn't noticed it until now: there was no music, no conversation, just the sound of running water, not like through the plumbing but the energetic coursing of subterranean rivers that reminded her that it had been a while since she'd washed, and yet she wasn't dirty, didn't smell bad—didn't smell at all.

What's going to happen, she wondered.

Then, making his way toward her from among the crowd, she saw a tall, thin man draped in a baggy leather jacket. He had protruding teeth that yellowed his enormous smile. He stopped in front of her.

Here. He held out a file. All taken care of.

Makina took the file and looked at its contents. There she was, with another name, another birthplace. Her photo, new numbers, new trade, new home. I've been skinned, she whispered.

When she looked up the man was no longer there and she tipped briefly into panic, she felt for a second—or for many seconds; she couldn't tell because she didn't have a watch, nobody had a watch—that the turmoil of so many new things crowding in on the old ones was more than she could take; but a second—or many—later she stopped feeling the weight of uncertainty and guilt; she thought back to her people as though recalling the contours of a lovely landscape that was now fading away: the Village, the Little Town, the Big Chilango, all those colors, and she saw that what was happening was not a cataclysm; she understood with all of her body and all of her memory, she truly understood, and when everything in the world fell silent finally said to herself I'm ready.

THE
TRANSMIGRATION
OF BODIES

For my mother, Irma Eugenia Gutiérrez Mejía

1

A scurvy thirst awoke him and he got up to get a glass of water, but the tap was dry and all that trickled out was a thin stream of dank air. Eyeing the third of mezcal on the table with venom, he got the feeling it was going to be an awful day. He had no way of knowing it already was, had been for hours, truly awful, much more awful than the private little inferno he'd built himself on booze. He decided to go out. He opened his door, was disconcerted not to see the scamper of la Ñora, who'd lived there since the days when the Big House was actually a Big House and not two floors of little houses—rooms for folks half-down on their luck—and then opened the front door and walked out. The second he took a step his back cricked to tell him something was off.

He knew he wasn't dreaming because his dreams were so unremarkable. If ever he managed to sleep several hours in a row, he dreamed, but his dreams were so lifelike they provided no rest: only small variations on his everyday undertakings and his everyday conversations and everyday fears. Occasionally his teeth fell out, but aside from that it was just everyday stuff. Nothing like this.

Buzzing: then a dense block of mosquitos tethering themselves to a puddle of water as tho attempting to lift it. There was no one, nothing, not a single voice, not one sound on an avenue that by that time should have been rammed with cars. Then he looked closer: the puddle began at the foot of a tree, like someone had leaned up against it to vomit. And what the mosquitos were sucking up wasn't water but blood.

And there was no wind. Afternoons it blew like a bitch so there should've at least been a light breeze, yet all he got was stagnation. Solid lethargy. Things felt much more present when they looked so abandoned.

He closed the door and stood there for a second not knowing what to do. He returned to his room and he stood there too, staring at the table and the bed. He sat on the bed. What worried him most was not knowing what to fear; he was used to fending off the unexpected, but even the unexpected had its limits; you could trust that when you opened the door every morning the world wouldn't be emptied of people. This, tho, was like falling asleep in an elevator and waking up with the doors open on a floor you never knew existed.

One thing at a time, he said to himself. First water. Then we'll figure out what the fuck. Water. He pricked up his nose and turned, attentive, to look around the place again and then said aloud Of course. He got up, went into the bathroom with a glass, pulled the lid off the tank and saw barely three fingers; he'd gotten up in the night to piss and the tank hadn't refilled after he flushed. He scraped the bottom with the glass but there was only enough for half. One drop of water was all that was left in his body and it had picked a precise place on his temple to bore its way out.

Fuckit, he said. Since when do I believe those bastards?

.   .   .

Four days ago their song and dance seemed like a hoax. Like the shock you feel when someone jumps out at you from behind a door and then says Relax, it's only me. Everyone was sure: if it was anything at all, it was no big shit. The disease came from a bug and the bug only hung around in squalid areas. You could swat the problem against the wall with a newspaper. Those too broke for a paper could use a shoe: no need to give them every little thing, after all. And *Too poor for shoes!* became the thing you spat at people who sneezed, coughed, swooned, or moaned O.

Only the ground floor of the Big House was actually inhabited, and of the inhabitants only the anemic student had actually been afraid. Once the warnings started he could be heard running to his door to spy through the peephole when anyone went in or out of the building. La Ñora certainly kept going out, keeping tabs on everyone on the block. And he'd seen Three Times Blonde go out one morning with her boyfriend. It unhinged him, having her so close, Three Times Blonde sleeping and waking and bathing only a wall and tiles away, Three Times Blonde pouring herself into itty-bitty sizes, her pantyline smiling at him as she walked off. She never noticed him at all, not even if they were leaving at the same time and he said Excuse me or You first or Please, except on one occasion when she was with her boyfriend and for a moment she'd not only turned to look at him but even smiled.

What did he expect, a man like him, who ruined suits the moment he put them on: no matter how nice they looked in shop windows, hanging off his bones they wrinkled in an instant, fell down, lost their grace. Ruined by the fetid stench of the courthouse. Or else his belongings just realized that his life was like a bus stop, useful for a moment but a place no one would stay for good. And she went for boyfriends like the one he'd seen—some slicked-back baby jack, four shirt buttons undone so everyone could see his gold virgin. The boyfriend had said hello, tho. Like the guy at the bar who tips on arrival so his drinks get poured with a heavy hand.

For the past four days the message had been Stay calm, everybody calm, this is not a big deal. On a bus, he himself had witnessed the pseudo-calm of skepticism: a street peddler had boarded the bus selling bottles of bubble gel; he blew into a plastic ring and little solar systems sailed down the aisle, oscillating, suspended, landing on people without bursting. Gel bubbles, he said, last far longer than soap bubbles, you can play with them, and he took a few between his fingers, jiggled, pressed, and puffed. One popped on a man's forehead. And just then the penny dropped: the bubble was full of air and spit from a stranger's mouth. A rictus of icy panic spread across the passengers' faces; the man got up and said Get the fuck off, the peddler stammered What's the problem, friend, no need to act like that, but the guy was already on him. When the guy lifted him up by his sweater the driver slowed—just a bit—and opened the doors so the vendor and his bottles could be tossed to the curb. Then he closed the doors and sped back up. And no one said a word. Not even him.

But at the time, they could still think they'd escaped the danger. Last night's news was no longer a dodge. The story had been picked up everywhere: two men in a restaurant, total strangers, started spitting blood almost simultaneously and collapsed over their tables. That was when the government came out and admitted: *We believe the epidemic*—and that was the first time they used the word—*may be a tad more aggressive than we'd initially thought, we believe it can only be transmitted by mosquitos*—EGYPTIAN mosquitos, they underscored—*tho there have been a couple of cases that appear to have been spread by other means, so while we are ruling out whatever we can rule out it's best to stop everything, tho really there's no cause for concern, we have the best and brightest tracking down whatever this is, and of course we have hospitals, too, but, just in case, you know, best to stay home and not kiss anybody or touch anybody and to cover your nose and your mouth and report any symptoms, but the main thing is Stay Calm.* Which, logically, was taken to mean Lock yourself up or this fucker will take you down, because we've unleashed some serious wrath.

He opened the Big House door again, took two steps out and was thrust back by the reek of abandonment on the street. Almost imperceptibly his frame flexed, anxious, updown updown, Fuckit fuckit fuckit, what do I do, and then he felt something brush his neck and he slapped his skin and looked at his hand, stained with insect blood. He stepped back, slammed the door and stood staring at his palm, transfixed.

What's going on? he heard behind him. He turned to see Three Times Blonde at the end of the hall. Half her body hanging out of her apartment, swinging from the jamb with one hand.

He took two steps toward her, wiping his hand on his pants. What's that? she asked.

Grease.

Three Times Blonde relaxed a bit and asked again.

What's going on out there?

Nothing, he replied. And I mean not a thing.

She nodded. She'd probably been watching the news without daring to believe it.

Good morning, he said.

Afternoon, you mean, Three Times Blonde fired back. She blinked silently at the ground, an outburst held in, and then added I got no credit on my phone.

Take some of mine, he offered immediately, as tho gravity itself forced him to say such things in the presence of a woman.

Three Times Blonde stood aside, and tho they could have done the deal in the hall she ticked her head toward her place. Her apartment gloried in its own good taste: purple love seat, poster of a blonde on an armchair not unlike the love seat, blue rug. He asked if he *might possibly* have a glass of water, thinking she was the sort who put stock in proper talk, but she just shot him a strange look.

They trafficked his time and she turned her back to make her call.

Three Times Blonde's pants rode her all over. He ogled her like she was in a window display, seized by the urge to devour her, to gorge himself on her thighs and her back and her tongue and then ask for her bones in a little bag to go. He pulled her blue pants down slow and trembling—but no, he didn't lift a finger; he inhaled the nape of her neck and kissed the three-times-blonde hair on it—but no, his hands stayed folded before him like the tea-sipping innocent he knew he could pass for. She was on the phone saying So what's going to happen, are we going to die or what? Then why won't you come over? But you have a car, you don't have to see a soul . . . Oh. And there's nobody that can stay with them? Whatever. Well if you don't come now it's going to get worse and then you really will be stuck there forever with your mother and your sisters, yeah, yeah, I know, it'll all be over soon, fine, okay, yeah, love you too, kiss-kiss.

She turned back around. He's not coming.

He should have taken off right then, should have said You're welcome—tho she hadn't said thanks—and split. But his will wasn't his own.

Let's watch TV, she said, and went into her bedroom.

He approached, not daring to cross the threshold. The room was pink and pillowed. She sat on the edge of the bed and turned on the TV and patted the mattress. Come.

Suddenly he began to salivate, his mouth no longer a desert with buzzards circling his tongue but a choking street, a flooded sewer. He obeyed and instructed himself to move no further. The newscaster on TV was talking about the airborne monster, its body a shiny striped black bullet, six very long fuzzy legs humped over itself, and above the hump a little round head with antennae casting out into space and two tubular mouths. A bona fide sonofabitch, apparently.

Looks pretty determined, don't you think? she asked.

He nodded yes and swallowed spit, then said But who knows if that's even the one, maybe they just found a fall guy, maybe this bug's taking the rap for another bug's dirtywork.

It was a joke, but Three Times Blonde turned to him wide-eyed and said You are so right it's scary.

163

She was convinced. Maybe it was true, maybe he was right.

Then the power went out. Three Times Blonde's apartment, just like his, got no natural light since they were at the back of the Big House, so suddenly it was dead of night. She said Yikes! and then fell silent, they both fell silent, a sensual silence, surreptitious: no need to do a thing. No need for phony swagger and no need to shoot her sidelong glances as if the door were half-open, just sit tight, knowing she's within kissing distance, even if no one else knows it and even if you can't prove it, it's a leap of faith.

So that was what it felt like: not always thinking about the moment to come, wasting each moment thinking about the moment to come, always the coming moment. So that was what it felt like to incubate, to settle in with yourself and hope the light stays off. And astonishingly, like a miracle, she said: I think this is what we were like before we were babies, don't you? Little larvae, sitting quietly in the dark.

He said nothing. Her voice had brought him back to the mattress, there in her pillowed room. Again he wanted to touch her and again he lacked someone to loan him the will.

You want a drink?

Oooh, yeah, I could go for a vodka.

I got mezcal.

He pictured her twisting her lips.

Well. You got to try everything once, right?

They got up off the bed and she placed one hand on his arm and one on his back.

Don't fall. If you conk out I won't be able to pick you up.

He let himself be led slower than necessary so she'd have to keep holding on. She opened the door and a square of light appeared from the small window in the door at the end of the hall.

Be right back.

He made it to the table in his apartment without fumbling, snatched up the bottle, and, with the skill of someone who's come home sloshed more than once, located the shot glasses. Before going back he walked to the end of the hall and looked out. He saw that the mosquitos had abandoned their puddle and what he'd thought was blood was in fact black floating scum. He recalled that on previous days he'd spotted several puddles covered in whitish membranes. This was the first black one he'd seen.

The city was still silent, overtaken by sinister insects.

On his way back he guided himself by the little inferno of her oven. The backlit blue silhouette of Three Times Blonde could be seen as she cut cheese, tomato and chipotle.

We're going to have something to eat, so I don't get silly when I drink.

They flipped and double-flipped and then folded the tortillas. Ate standing up. Then began to drink.

So how come nobody ever comes to visit you? she asked.

Everyone's fine right where they are, he replied. And me and mezcal don't talk shop.

Lonely people lose their minds, she said.

He always found it a miracle that anyone wanted his company. Women especially—men will cuddle a rock. When he first started getting laid he couldn't quite believe that the women in his bed weren't there by mistake. Sometimes he'd leave the room and then peer back in, and then peer in again, incredulous that a woman was actually lying there naked, waiting for him. As if. In time he found his thing: fly in like a fool to start, then turn on the silver tongue. Talk and cock, talk and cock, yessir. One time a girl confessed that Vicky, his friend the nurse, had given her a warning before she introduced them. Take one look and if you don't like what you see don't even say hi or you'll end up wanting to fuck. Best thing anyone ever said about him. It didn't matter that they never came back, or rarely. He didn't mind being disposable.

Three Times Blonde told him about her family. About a brother she never saw since he was a bad drunk and a hophead and when he was off his face he said awful things. About her mother, who introduced her to guys from work. Total scum. To illustrate what these people were like, honestly, she described their defining details: a lawyer from the office who would jam a napkin up his gums after eating and then put it back on the table, or this one guy who could never sit still and would readjust himself every other second saying, *I swear, my balls are just too damn big.*

Can you imagine? she asked. I mean these people. Honestly.

His type of people. Those were his kind, the kind he rubbed shoulders with, did deals with every day, the *nous* of his *entre nous*, his tribe.

Which is why it's so wondrous, he thought, why it's so weird, to be this close to her when we're from such different dirt. As Three Times Blonde spoke the whole house echoed in the absence of noise from outside, and for a minute he felt that now, really, all they had was time, and he got a good kind of creeps and was flooded with a patience he didn't know he possessed. But then she started talking about her boyfriend, as if he was different from all the others, If only you knew him. And using a new sound as an excuse he said Be right back, and went out into the hall.

He opened the door. There stood the anemic student, hunched, pale, dank hair dripping down his forehead like dirty bathwater. No doubt the guy hadn't ventured out in days and the smell of quesadillas had gotten to him. For a second he considered saying Come on in, compadre, fix you something right up. If he'd been another class of man or arrived at another class of time he would have, but all he said was Go home, you'll catch cold. He closed the door and went back to Three Times Blonde. Ha.

Three Times Blonde had put out a couple scented candles and was kicking it in the purple den. He poured her a second mezcal and they toasted, did it right, eyes on the shot glass—none of this staring into one another's eyes as if already wounded—and he downed it in one. Mezcal, so good so true. Distilled filth to filter his filth inside. He slammed the glass on the table and poured a third. Shots made him a better man: his teeth whitened, his wit quickened, his stiff hair stayed kempt and acted like it gave a shit. She didn't need it, of course, she was rosy-cheeked and graceful sans hoodwinkery, but she too downed hers in one. I always assumed mezcal was slimy since they make it with dead worms, she said. And him: No, the worm is what gives it life.

Like the nose on a u, she said.

Mmm?

You know how it has those two dots when it really sounds like u?

Dieresis.

The nose on a u. When it's with a q the u doesn't breathe, only when it's far from q, and it doesn't need a nose there. But I always put one on anyway.

She traced the letter in the air with one finger and dotted it. Like that.

He poured her one more and this time they did look into each other's eyes before down-the-hatching. She glistened like a wet street. This might be the last woman I'm ever with in my life, he said to himself. He said that every time because, like all men, he couldn't get enough, and because, like all men, he was convinced he deserved to get laid one more time before he died.

A flat silence slipped in from outside, the hours on the street withering in abandonment, while those in the house were watered in mezcal. But the mezcal was running low.

He had an emergency bottle at home. But what if the anemic student was there, curled up by the door waiting for them to toss him a tortilla. He was determined to hold out until the bastard had slunk back to his doghouse.

Sometimes I go outside in the middle of the night, said Three Times Blonde. If there's not much light you can see the stars. No way we can do that now.

He looked up a lot too, nights when he was still on the grind at dawn and the streets were deserted. But he kept that quiet, she'd never buy it.

So you were telling me about Prince Charming, he said; and she said Foo don't be mean.

He's very refined, she said. This is my first boyfriend, my first really real one.

Then she started saying she'd met him at a party, fighting to defend the honor of a girl being bothered by two drunks and she fell head over heels just like that; okay, she admitted, he's a bit cocky, and yeah he sometimes raises his voice, and sure he's insanely jealous and sometimes drinks a lot and fusses too much over Bronco—

Who's Bronco?

His car, silly.

He named his car?

Yeah, see he takes such good care of it. But when it's just the two of us alone together he is so sweet, if you could only see him.

Good grief. Little slickster, alias Angelface.

Something in the air swished a candle, flicking light onto Three Times Blonde's shoulder and suddenly he envisioned her unwrapped. Without thinking his hand reached out and very gently squeezed.

We went to the beach last week, she said, looking at him like he wasn't touching her.

With the other hand he turned her slightly and began, ever so softly, to squeeze more as her skin surrendered.

Mmm, that feels nice, she said. Keep doing that.

He kept doing it, inwardly faster and outwardly keener, with a tremble he fought by staring only at his next little crest of flesh. And then he began with his mouth. Just peeling off the wrapper and popping each little crest into his mouth. She cocked her head slightly to glance from the corner of her eye and said You are insane, you know that? He said Nnnf and kept at it.

When he got to her shoulder blade he came upon a scar like a line upturned at the ends, deep. He traced it with one finger.

How'd you get that?

My fucking deranged brother. When we were kids one day he lost his shit and tried to knife me with a spoon.

A spoon?

I'm telling you he's deranged.

He stopped touching the scar carefully, as tho afraid it might come off, and kissed it. She arched her back. He pulled down one spaghetti strap but before peeling off the rest traced his fingertips along the sierra of her spine. No longer leaning over to squeeze small folds of her, he slid across as if his arms were too short and he had to scoot right up to reach. As he kneaded another knot, almost to the edge of her back, he lowered the other hand to her hip and pulled her to him gently. For the first time she tensed.

You and me don't even know each other.

He stopped moving his hands but didn't take them off or release the pressure on her hip.

That's the best part, he said.

And even before he said what he said next, he could tell the bastard was back. Bastard alias the Romantic.

It's the best part, because affection is exactly what we need. Can you imagine what it would be like if instead of killing we cuddled? You seen how many people are out there hurting each other without even knowing who they're shooting at?

He believed that, he really did, and yet he was still a bastard because he'd said it like a man paying off the popo to disappear a ticket. Obviously he couldn't let this chance slip by. But still: bastard.

Three Times Blonde turned to look at him like he'd said something unforgivable. She stared tremulously a couple of seconds, then pulled him in by the neck and kissed him, sweeping her tongue across his as if surveying a new possession, marking more than kissing him, and he, already overexcited, had no idea what to do, but his left hand, which had twisted with her waist, and his right hand, which had landed on her belly, lent him the will that had wavered. He slipped his hands beneath her top and uncovered her breasts. They weren't like he'd imagined them, with his hands and his head, so many times: they're never the way you imagine them, they were smaller and pointier and one was slightly inverted as tho ordering him to suck it out, and as he obeyed he was shocked that Three Times Blonde started taking off his shirt, that she wanted it too.

He frenzied from breast to breast, undone by the inability to tongue them both at the same time. He licked his way down the almost-invisible trail of three-times-blonde peach fuzz that crept into her pants, which he unbuttoned, but before pulling them off he slipped a hand through her thong to finger her curls. He stood, fearful in that half-second she'd be overcome with ambivalence as he took off his own pants, but she was already stroking his stomach with the tip of one toe. He dropped everything but his unsexy underwear, knelt, and as he started to tug her panties aside heard Three Times Blonde ask What's my name?

He raised his head, racing breakneck through half-a-dozen idiotic replies.

Like you know mine.

That's not the same, you swine.

He'd had the good sense not to stop moving his fingers for the duration of that exchange and by the end Three Times

Blonde had stopped worrying about names and he let his tongue revel the way a tongue can only revel when nobody's asking it for words. As soon as he sensed he didn't need further permission he pulled off her panties and got naked and pulled her to him by the hips but then she said Where's the condom?

Motherfuck the condom. He'd asked himself the same thing and had answered himself Don't fuckin worry about it right now.

He put his pants back on, said Don't move.

He stepped into the hall barefoot. The anemic student was nowhere to be seen.

He ran into his apartment reciting the prayer of the over-heated horndog:

> Oh please, oh please, oh please
> May he, the drunken me
> May he, the dumbfuck me
> May he, the me who never ever ever knows where shit is
> May he have saved one
> Just one
> Lubricated or corrugated
> Colored or flavored
> Magnum or tight-fit
> Oh please
> Holy Saint of horndogs
> Grant me just one condom

But he knew there were none. He'd used that prayer the last time, months ago, and managed to unearth one under the bed, gleaming and glorious as a national hero. The very last one. This was not a time for heroes or miracles. Fear was what had granted him these hours of intimacy but now it was showing its virulent side. Go on, off to the shop, ladykiller.

Across the street was an old-school pharmacy run by little old men who still wrapped condoms and sanitary napkins in brown paper so the customer need not feel self-conscious on the way out, but in the mental photo he'd taken that morning the metal awning was down. He triangulated the hood in his head, locating shops and less-far pharmacies and said to himself, Be right back, no big deal. He walked out of his place and before walking back into Three Times Blonde's saw the anemic student at the end of the hall, staring at him, fiery-eyed, glassy, on his way out the door.

Three Times Blonde was still splayed across the love seat, transfixed by the shadows cast by the candle. He told her what he'd told himself:

Be right back, there's a pharmacy close by.

She sat straight up on the couch.

No no no, how could you leave with that thing out there, it's not like we're that desperate.

Evidently she knew nothing about him. In other circumstances he wouldn't have listened, but the current circumstance, the one that concerned him, wasn't the epidemic so much as Three Times Blonde herself, naked before him, adamant, insisting Come. That was all. No pharmacies and no condoms. Locked up with a woman who was calling him.

Like a wrestler, he said to himself, I surrender. He approached and attacked her tongue as he once more undressed and then she said We can't get comfy out here and led him into the bedroom where at first she just let him adore her unwrapped three-times-very-taut skin and run his lips across it and his fingers inside it, but then she put her mouth to his cock, no talk; they rolled around clutching bony and fleshy backs, round and skinny buttocks, until there in the center of it all he felt her so wet and so ready and so present that he just slid inside. It was worth it, no matter the price, just to feel her drawing his cock in from the deepest part of her body, even if only for an instant. He did it fast but in that time a million epidemics came and went, through a million deserted cities in which the only sounds were deep sighs, and then she, once more, looked at him like he'd done something unforgiveable, a thing that for one very long minute he did not want to end: she trapped him with the lips of her sex, with her legs, with her fingernails, and then said, in a steady but almost inaudible voice, Off.

He pulled out and slumped beside her. He thought she'd kick him out and told himself the same thing he'd told himself so many times in so many situations: All good things are but a part of something terrible. But instead of shouting at him she reached out a hand and took hold of his cock, squeezing and stroking steadily until he came, tho he begged Wait wait wait, stop, because he had his hopes set on who knows what.

He dreamed. Among the succession of images in his dream, a replay of his half-assed hungover day, was one of a black dog who turned up often; this time the black dog, shaggy and wet, was shaking himself energetically, whipping out shards of water like little sliced-up lakes, and with each sliver that flew off he felt himself—since the dog was also him—grow lighter, lighter, lighter, lighter, until he awoke so light he could touch the ceiling.

She was still there beside him. Not once in the night had he lost awareness that she was there. Not when he was an animal shooting out shards of water, not in the flickering light at the end of the hallway, not in the face of the anemic student staring at him one last time before he left, had he ever stopped knowing she was there, spooning him. Yet he told himself anyway: there they were, the two of them, at the same lock-in under the same roof.

He started stroking her from curve to curve. He heard the fridge start up behind the door and panicked. The power had come back on and he feared she might flip the lights and see him, squalid, ruining her mattress the way he ruined suits, so when he felt her start to stir he said Shh shh shh and slipped a gentle hand between her thighs to rouse her sex softly, awaken it gently. He moved his hand ever so lightly and as he did she moaned, and he moved a little more and felt his sorrow start to slip away and himself finally defeat what his roughneck cousins used to say to one another if they saw a drop-dead gorgeous girl: Ain't nothin the likes of you could do with the likes of that.

He felt her body contract and release and then languish again, but awake now.

Bet you can't do that, she said after a minute.

What?

See colors like I do. When I was a girl it was just bright lights but now I see colored lights.

What colors did you see just now?

I don't know. They were pastel. When they go out I forget.

This was exactly the way he wanted everything to stay. Let them bury me, he said to himself, let them scatter dirt on me, mouth wide open, snuggled up just like this. Let them bury me. Let them burn me and turn me, mark me and merk me. They can deep-six me if they want, but let everything stay like this.

Suddenly, like an involuntary twitch: guilt.

I meant what I said yesterday, he declared. I said it to sway you but I meant what I said.

She said nothing.

You mad?

That stuff about how great it'd be if the world was all loved up?

Yes.

Pfft, I knew that. What, you think I'm stupid? That's just a way to flirt, right? Why bring it up now? Silly.

Why indeed. She was right.

It's just habit, tricks of the trade, but I didn't want it to be like that with you. You know what I do?

Yes.

He sat up, and it was he who turned on the little bedside lamp to look at her.

You do? For real?

Of course. You're a fixer. Take care of stuff under the table at the courts.

He froze. For her to call him that, after all those kisses.

One time I heard la Ñora say The landlord told me not to bother the guy in 3 if he's late with the rent—that man knows a lot of people and he doesn't want any trouble.

He said nothing, but the silence was interrupted by his phone. He decided to answer. Like a man who goes to the john to sidestep the bill.

He picked up and said Yeah. No one spoke but he knew the half-lung wheezy sonofabitch on the other end of the line, and knew if he was calling now, with the city shut down the way it was, that he was needed and couldn't say no.

Who's this? the man asked, like he didn't know what number he'd just dialed.

Who do you think, replied the Redeemer. It's me.

2

Animals. They behave like animals, the Redeemer thought, watching a line of cats prowl the ledges along the block, and a small happy dogpack trot down the center of the street; they wagged their tails and cocked their ears, sneezed loudly, and when a car came along they parted with careful coordination before chasing it a few feet, barking at the tires. They're more clever when there's nothing in the way, he thought. The air seemed almost insubordinate with odors: because there was no smoke, the scent of jacaranda could be clearly discerned among the miasmas that had been blown uphill like never before, in the tropical storm that had skewiffed the wind like never before—and so the smells, rather than fading, fermented.

There were a few people out and about, but more like ephemeral grubs than lords of the land. A few in cars with the windows rolled up. In a park three blocks away, the man who used to predict the end of days, now alone, in silence, thrown off. A guy in a white robe crossing the street with quick steps. And pharmacies, two-bit pharmacies, open. The Redeemer stopped in one to buy facemasks and a bottle of water. The salesgirl served him from a disgusted distance and took his coins one by one through a handkerchief.

This doesn't seem so bad, the Redeemer thought, almost happy. Long as it doesn't last. And suddenly he no longer hated Dolphin quite so much for having hauled him from the bed of Three Times Blonde, who'd said Who in hell would order you out on a day like this? and pointed to the street. And he'd said An asshole with exceptional timing, and as she watched him get dressed she'd said You are seriously nuts, and then added: We were having fun, you and me, and now I'll have to lock the door when you come back knocking. The Redeemer had stopped buttoning his shirt a second to see if she meant it, and tho he could see that she did he'd kept doing up his buttons and said Don't know about you, but I make my living off the places people can't get out of.

Just then he hadn't wanted to get out of anything, particularly, yet his reflexes kicked in the second the phone rang and Dolphin said I need you to help me with a swap.

For who?

For me.

What happened?

Don't know. Shit went down last night. Someone took my son.

Romeo?

Yeah.

Of course he knew who had him, that was why he'd called. Not to locate the kid but to get him back. So who did Dolphin have? Who'd he want to exchange him for?

Where'd this go down? he asked.

Lover's Lane, said Dolphin.

The Bug eyed him with a distinct lack of urgency, as if to say You think I give a shit about epidemics? No car stares straight at you the way a Bug does, he thought. It was the most expressive thing on the block. The Redeemer got in and drove across the city to see what he could wheedle out of Óscar, a compadre of his who worked the bar at a cathouse. Lover's Lane was home to eight brothels in total, and together they tended to the various sectors of the population. There was one had cachet for kingpins and thugs with serious bank—even served champagne, and was staffed by girls who, word was, had appeared on soap operas. Two for those who liked to think they were street but lived nowhere near it, and tho those joints didn't splash out on pricey juice or fine females, at least they could keep the lights on. Four itty-bitty bordellos with classic red-light decor and cement floors for the roughnecks, who also had the right to kick back. And a big old tomcathouse for women who earned their own dough: disco ball on the ceiling, tiger-skin sofas, and strippers with huge muscles and tiny G-strings, ready to romp for the right price. Óscar worked at Metamorphosis, where the better-bred boys went once in a while to put hair on their chests. Next door was Incubus—the one for women—so Óscar always had hot tips on what was going down on Lover's Lane.

He found him standing at the entry, stroking his tash as he gazed down the empty street. The Redeemer was embarrassed to be wearing a mask and considered taking it off for a minute, but opted to leave it on.

How goes it, Óscar, my man?

It don't, Counselor, as you can see for yourself.

Óscar was one of the only people he could stand calling him that.

The Redeemer pokerfaced: You know the whereabouts of Romeo Fonseca?

Dolphin's boy?

Mhm.

Óscar had looked into the Redeemer's eyes and then stared down the street again, stroking his tash with a don't-know-jack face: obviously the Redeemer was about to ask him something and he was going to tell but it had to be clear he was not one to simply offer stuff up.

He was here last night, right?

Óscar nodded almost imperceptibly, like it was the natural extension of his tash-tugging.

He started off somewhere else—nodding now toward Incubus—then showed up here; after that I don't know.

The Redeemer let his true question ripen in the silence of the street.

Didn't see where but you saw who with.

Óscar finally took his hand off his face and pointed to a spot on the sidewalk, as tho conjuring the scene with his fingers.

Only thing I saw was him sprawled there. Couple kids came and put him in a van.

Kids, what kids?

The Castros.

The Castros, the Redeemer thought. Motherfuck.

How'd Dolphin find out?

You still on that prick's payroll? Óscar asked.

In his line, people fell all over themselves to say thanks if he fixed their situations, nearly wept with joy when he kept their hands clean of certain matters, they sent small checks and big bottles in gratitude. After that, tho, they didn't even want to say hey since it reminded them of what they'd been mixed up in. Maybe that was how he felt about Dolphin: just hearing the sound of that agonized wheeze reminded him of that one defining moment he tried to keep buried. But the Redeemer had never stopped repaying the man who'd stepped in to lend a hand at a rough time.

Still on it.

Mmm... well. Must've heard because his girl was here too.

The Redeemer eyed him, alarmed.

His daughter? The Unruly?

In the flesh. Up to her eyeballs she was, coming out of Incubus, saw it all go down but didn't say shit till after they took her sib, then screamed her head off, tho no one seemed to notice.

The Redeemer nodded. He pulled out the masks he had in his pocket, held on to one and handed the rest to Óscar.

These of any use to you?

Everything's of use to me here, he replied.

He drove back to his side of town, which was also where the Fonsecas were, some six blocks up the hill from the Big House. On the way he saw a train go by. Trains almost never went by anymore since they'd been sold off years back. But here was a convoy of eight sealed cars advancing slowly along the tracks. Carrying out the healthy or the sick? he wondered.

He parked in front of their big sheet-metal gate and slapped it ten times in a row so they'd hear him in the house, which stood beyond the slapdash patio that Dolphin had erected for parties. No one came. He beat on the gate ten more times and waited. Nada. He was about to start slapping again when he heard a bolt slide on the other side of the entryway.

Who's that? a girl's voice banged out. Her.

It's me, he said.

The Unruly said nothing, but the Redeemer could hear her breathing through the metal.

Your pops called.

The girl undid a second bolt and showed half an unfriendly face through the doorcrack—brow arched, nose wrinkled, mouth twisted. She said nothing. The Redeemer repeated Your pops called for me. Go ask him.

Don't you tell me what I can or can't do, spat the Unruly. She stared at him and then closed the door. After five minutes, she returned. Come back later, she said. Not right now.

The Redeemer snorted but didn't move, nor did the Unruly close the door.

Who'd you grab? he asked. Please not who he thought, please not who he thought.

The Unruly narrowed her eyes and said Baby Girl.

Shit. But that wasn't what he said. What he said was Where you got her?

The Unruly gave a sort of half-smile that said You must be kidding.

Why bother calling if you give me nothing to go on, he persisted, I'm not going to do anything, but I need to get an angle on this.

The Unruly pressed her face up to the half-open door. She smelled of brandy.

Real close. In that big white house. Cross from the elementary school.

Odd. The Redeemer prided himself on knowing about all the palmgreasing, hornswoggling, and machinating in the city, but this house had him stumped. Who owned Las Pericas? And why would Dolphin hide Baby Girl there?

Okay, he said, I'll be around, tell your pops to call me.

The Unruly slammed the door, and he listened to her walk away.

He got a text from the government assuring him that everything would be back to normal any minute now, that it was essential to exercise extreme caution but not to panic: a reassuring little pat on the head to say Any silence is purely coincidental, okay? Like when people are talking and everyone goes quiet, like when an angel passes, like that. But it came off more like Better to play down than stir up.

Baby Girl. The Redeemer recalled the first time he'd met Baby Girl on a job he did for her dad: itty-bitty thing, quiet, long hair always carefully brushed, pretty face but eyes so sad. The kind of girl you wanted to love, really truly, but then the urge passed kind of fast. Even for her family. The Redeemer had seen it, at a big blowout after that job, seen the way they treated her like a piece of furniture from another era, one you hold onto even tho it's uncomfortable. The Castros had been putting on airs for years and Baby Girl cramped their style. Now the Fonsecas, too, had struck it rich, but about style they couldn't care less. So different and so the same, the Castros and the Fonsecas. Poor as dirt a couple decades ago, now too big for their boots, and neither had moved out of the barrio: they just added locks and doors and stories and a shit-ton of cement to their houses, one with more tile than the other. So different and so the same. If he thought about it, in all these years he'd never once seen them cross each other.

Until now. Odd for them to butt heads right when there was finally enough room.

But he'd seen this before, the way old grudges resurface. Even in this city, where people didn't nose around, no matter what was done or who was doing it, sometimes it could almost seem like We're all one. Don't matter if your thing's a burning bush, some lusty dove, a buried book, big bank, talk or cock, there's room for us all. But no sir, he knew better, the real deal was: Don't give a shit what you're doing but you better not look at me, fucker. Every once in a while people did look; every once in a while they remembered what they'd seen. But man, for this all to go down now—just when everyone and their mother was cowering under the bed?

He passed by the local park once more. The grass on the median looked overgrown tho it had only been ignored a couple of days. Inside the park, in a little fountain where a colony of frogs used to live, he saw none; the water was dead, bereft of ripples; for a second he considered bending down to drink from it because he'd only bought one bottle and finished it, but opted instead to walk another block to the pharmacy.

The pharmacy was closed. On the metal shutter a piece of paper: *Out of Masks.*

He'd been told, that time, to go get Baby Girl from some corner store in a barrio stuck on the side of the hill. A boyfriend had tried to abduct her, but at a traffic light she got out of the car and ran into the shop. The boyfriend followed but when he tried to drag her out, the owners chased him off and someone called one of Baby Girl's brothers—yes, everyone knows fucking everyone. Before the brothers could head out to butcher the boyfriend, tho, their father stopped them, calling in the Redeemer to keep it from escalating into a major shitstorm. The boyfriend wasn't on juice, or blow, or smack, he just couldn't stand Baby Girl getting feisty and refusing to go with him when he'd made up his mind. The Redeemer got to the corner store, made sure Baby Girl was okay, and she was—pallor and little-lamb panting were as much a part of her as eye-color—then went to sweet-talk lover boy.

Hey, hey, amigo, listen up a minute. I got no dog in this fight, okay, I just want to say one thing and I'll be on my way. Cool? Listen, man, I'm with you, I know what it's like—respect, that's what it's all about, and it's your girl those lowlifes got socked away in there, not theirs, right? Thing is, tho, people don't see you been disrespected if you don't make a fuss. Times it's better to let things slide and come off like a king, comprende? All I'm sayin, a badass ain't the one to raise his voice but the one with no need to—just think on it. And the boyfriend not only thought on it but thanked him and heartily shook his hand before shouting into the store: But we ain't through, Baby! And sure enough, two weeks later they were back together. That was no longer his problem. The Redeemer sweet-talked only as much as he had to. Let people get in all the tight spots they want; he'd be out of a job if he started passing judgment on their vices. That same night, when he took Baby Girl home, each time he asked her what the boyfriend had done, she said Nothing, señor, honest, I just didn't want to go with him.

He helped the man who let himself be helped. Often, people were really just waiting for someone to talk them down, offer a way out of the fight. That was why when he talked sweet he really worked his word. The word is ergonomic, he said. You just have to know how to shape it to each person. One time this little gaggle of teenage boys had gone to the neighbor's on the other side of the street and stoned the windows and kicked the door for a full half-hour, shouting Come on out, motherfucker, we'll crack your skull, and the pigs hadn't deigned to appear; that was one of the first times the Redeemer had done his job. He went out, asked in surprise how it was they'd yet to bust down the door and added You want, I'll bring you out a pickax right now, and that sure calmed them down; see, it's one thing to front, to act like a big thing, but burning bridges, well that's a whole 'nother thing. Soon as he saw what was what the Redeemer added: Tho, really, why even bother, right? Man's in there shitting himself right now, and they all laughed and they all left. That was when the Redeemer learned that his talent lay not so much in being brutal as in knowing what kind of courage every fix requires. Being humble and letting others think the sweet words he spoke were in fact their own. It worked on others but not on him. He'd met politicians who could believe whatever came out of their mouths as long as others believed it too. He tried to learn how but could never forget lies. Especially his own.

He trusted Dolphin—or trusted him as much as anyone who'd been a buzzman for twenty-five years can be trusted—but the Las Pericas thing was prickling his neckhairs. What was up with that? He decided to ask Gustavo, a sharp-witted lawyer who knew the ropes and had been untying the city's secrets for decades. He called, but a woman's voice said he wasn't in and who knew when he'd be back.

He needed someone to watch his back. He called the Neeyanderthal and climbed back in the Bug to go get him.

The Neeyanderthal was an entrepreneur of sorts: it was all bidness for the Neeyanderthal. Everywhere you look, he liked to say, looks like wheels and deals. He bought old cell phones that he sold at new prices to credulous clients, organized office pools at places he didn't work, and shuffled the cash flow to keep all his balls in the air: he smuggled shit in, sold intel, rented his house out as a place for petty crimes to go down. He never had any money. Instead his rackets seemed designed to prove he was cleverer than everyone else, to bring him doses of euphoria followed by stretches of contained rage. The Neeyanderthal was huge and hulking, a man who walked like he was forever on his way out of the ICU, moving each muscle with considerable care.

Years ago the Neeyanderthal's brother had died in his arms, on the way back from a nearby town: some kid had crossed the road in front of them, the Neeyanderthal jammed on the brakes, the brother flew through the windshield, the truck flipped and by the time the Neeyanderthal could get out from under it, his baby brother was dying on the white line and kept right on dying even as the Neeyanderthal held his face, sobbing into it saying Hold on, man, almost there little brother, as tho that could extend his life. It didn't. Finally the ambulance came to pick up the body, by then so lulled and soothed it looked almost at peace.

To the Redeemer it seemed the Neeyanderthal had been trying to off himself on blow for years. After the brother thing he launched into more honest attempts. Provoking police, street fighting. Then one time while he was truly looped he came right out and tried to shoot himself through the heart. Like it was no big deal, people were at his place getting trashed, and he got up, went to his room and fired a shot. His luck was so bad one of the credit cards he kept in his pocket to cut coke deflected the bullet, which flew up, barely kissed the top of his heart and came out his back. They found him standing unsteadily with a lost look on his face. Guess this ain't a boneyard kind of day, he said, and claimed he was smiling when he said it.

The Redeemer had never contemplated suicide, not even the time Dolphin had pulled him out of that black hole. Whenever he heard about someone who'd decided to cut their own life short he was shocked, especially if it was someone who had the strength to defend themselves; it surprised him not because he thought it was wrong but because he suddenly saw that person like they belonged to an entirely different species, and was astonished they inhabited the same planet. People who could make decisions they weren't prepared for. So you want to inhale ammonia? You fuckin sure? Dead silence.

He got to the Neeyanderthal's place, rang the bell and went back to the Bug to wait.

He watched a junkman pull his cart up the middle of the street. The junkman looked at the Redeemer in his mask, smiled with superiority, began hacking dramatically, then shook his head side to side and kept on his way.

The door opened.

What's up, Neeyan? asked the Redeemer.

Damn, man, not a tail to chase or a soul in sight, said the Neeyanderthal, staring out the Bug's window at the empty streets.

The Redeemer crossed an avenue with two military trucks down it and turned in another direction.

First time there's no traffic and I still got to take the long way, he said.

At the next avenue they caught sight of a very small funeral procession: one hearse with two cars following behind, three people in the first car, only one in the last.

Oh, yeah, said the Neeyanderthal, looks like people are real choked up over this fuckin corpse.

Passing the procession the Neeyanderthal stuck his head out and said aloud, as if addressing the body in the hearse, You're fooling yourself, man, you're fooling yourself.

He would say that about anything: a political argument, a lover's secret, a soccer game. Afterward he'd add something smartass; in this case, once his head was back inside the Bug, he said Should've vacuum-packed your ass . . .

Dependable as gravity, that was the Neeyanderthal. He messed with everyone like it was an obligation. Why was he the Neeyanderthal's compadre? Was it because they'd once been real friends? Was it that he'd watched him grow sadder and sadder? Or that in him he saw something of his own black dog? That's why we make enemies of our friends as soon as they start to drift, he thought, cos that way they get stuck with all our flaws, unlike when they're shared. Maybe brief friendships are best. If you pull out in time, the vices are all theirs.

Close to his barrio the Redeemer turned and found himself head-on with another military truck. This time he couldn't dodge it so he braked slowly and started a U-turn but a soldier waved him to where he should stop. He parked the Bug and waited. The soldier approached the car, peered into the back seat, then at the Redeemer and finally at the Neeyanderthal, who said What? I didn't hear anything about a curfew. Can't a man go out anymore without catching shit?

The soldier walked around to the Neeyanderthal's side and stared at him with no expression, making no attempt to bend down. Then he glanced back to the truck and nodded toward the Bug. A masked officer approached and ordered the Redeemer out with an index finger. He got out. Another soldier was patting down a punk rocker, palms against the truck.

Good morning, Captain, the Redeemer said.

The captain's eyebrows arched almost imperceptibly, seeming to indicate an appreciation for the Redeemer's knowledge of rank. But what he said was: Afternoon, you mean.

The captain stared at him as tho chewing a twig. Patient, reflective. The Redeemer realized he'd do well to keep quiet and silently composed his best body language to say: You say jump, Captain, I'll ask how high. The captain glanced sidelong at the Neeyanderthal and said Couple of smartasses, I see.

The Redeemer half-closed his eyes in apology.

Captain, I can't even imagine what you must have to put up with in a situation like this, the thing is, sir, we're all uneasy, as you can imagine, and the only thing we really want is to get home and lock ourselves up.

At the truck, one of the soldiers had pushed the punk against the hood and spat The fuck is all this crap you got on?, slapping his ears, his lip, where he wore rings. The boy accepted the slaps without raising his hands.

Going to have to take you in and do background checks, the captain said.

But suddenly he'd stopped looking at the Redeemer: he turned his attention to the soldiers by the truck and said Take that shit off him. One of the soldiers cuffed the kid's hands behind him and the other began to rip out the rings. The punk writhed in silence, trails of blood starting to run from his eyebrows, his nose, his mouth. The Redeemer sensed this was his chance to dig a hole in the wall and sneak out. Another day he'd have tried to help the kid, but today it was a no-go.

Any chance you could do me a favor, officer? I certainly don't want to take up any more of your time.

He took out one of the business cards that boasted a degree he'd never earned and said In case I can ever be of any service to you.

The captain took the card but didn't turn to look at it. He waited a couple seconds, then with his left index finger sent him back to the Bug, and with his right ordered the soldiers to put the punk in the truck. Thank you, Captain, the Redeemer said. He got into the car and started the engine.

They drove several blocks in silence and then the Neeyanderthal said Dude was asking for it, right? You walk around like a faggot, all that metal in your face, you pay the price.

And the Redeemer replied Shut up.

Go to Las Pericas, said the text from a number he didn't know, but it could only have been Dolphin.

With some people it was hard to take the measure of their mettle till you saw them in a very tight squeeze. With

Dolphin there wasn't much mystery. Ex-buzzman, divorced, one son and one daughter. He'd earned his nickname when he burned a hole in his nose snorting too much blow; as if that wasn't enough, he then got shot in the chest and could now only breathe through one lung. Even so he managed to act like these were still the days when he wore a tin star, carried chrome, slapped people around on the street. Still: the Redeemer wasn't expecting to hear him say what he said when he went to see Baby Girl.

He got to Las Pericas with the Neeyanderthal, and the Unruly was already waiting outside.

Only one goes in, she said as soon as she saw the Neeyanderthal, and tell this guy to put on a mask or get the fuck out of here.

The Redeemer handed Neeyan a mask, which he used to wipe his mouth, like it was a napkin, and then threw on the ground. The Unruly's little eyes shone like she was smiling.

Go on in, she said to the Redeemer.

The Las Pericas place was huge and white with a big wooden veranda, as if someone had been unwilling to give up their old house in the tropics, despite now living on a hill a thousand klicks from the sea. This was the first time the Redeemer had ever been inside. As soon as he stepped through the door he was dazzled by a huge room with a dozen high windows. In the center stood a table, and on the table lay Baby Girl.

He didn't need to get close to know Baby Girl was no longer all there, but still he had to do it, and to look after what was left. He approached reluctantly, his steps slow, as tho in place of bones he had a barbed-wire soul. He saw Baby

Girl there, pale, ashen, a trail of blood between her nose and mouth, hands clenched and face exceedingly sad. She was so small and so still, but at the same time seemed like the heart of the house, cold yet somehow keeping it alive. Who knew how many dead bodies he'd seen, but this one reminded him too much of the other one, his one.

That was when Dolphin appeared behind the Redeemer, and said—there in the brightest room in the world, pointing to the loneliest girl in existence—I still got it. They try to fuck me over? I still got it.

This job would be easy if the only ones we had to fight were our friends, the Redeemer used to say, but what he said to himself now was I don't want to listen to this motherfucker, and I do not even want to think about the eye-for-an-eye bullshit, the tooth-for-a-toothery this is going to unleash. On other occasions he'd convinced himself that even the most twisted men deserve a chance, since people, all people, are like dark stars: what we see is different from the thing itself, which has already disappeared, already changed, even a single second after the light or evil has been discharged. But this . . .

What did you do to her?

Nothing new, said Dolphin.

Why here? Why you got her here?

Not your concern, asshole, said the Dolphin patting his head, not your concern. You seen her, now get to work.

The Redeemer felt in his gut the desire to wrench off what nose Dolphin had left but the rest of his body couldn't carry out the order. He turned and walked out of the house. Outside, the Neeyanderthal was talking to the Unruly.

So, what line are you in, sweetness?

The Unruly was on the verge of saying something different but when she saw the Redeemer her look hardened and she said, Revenge.

The Redeemer held her gaze and contained the urge to take her by the shoulders and shake her. He ought to have done it, ought to have beat Dolphin till not his nose but his whole face was destroyed, if he wanted to salvage any vestige of himself. Behind his back he heard Dolphin approach laboriously and say Don't pay her any mind. This ain't about getting revenge, just about getting even.

3

What do you mean am I sure? Vicky retorted after the Redeemer asked if she'd go with him. Shit, you've already been out on the street with the Neeyanderthal, right? But did you ask him if he was sure he wanted to go? No. Right, asshole? Dumbass can't shoot for shit, can't hit himself with his own damn gun, and there you are dragging him all over town, but me, who takes care of every fucking thing under the sun for a living, I'm some little señorita that needs your protection.

He couldn't help it, it wasn't an attempt at gallantry, just came with the job: in the Kingdom of the Word all men were Chiefs and all women Lil' Ladies, as far as he was concerned, and tho he was well aware that Vicky was not only nail-hard by nature but also an adrenaline junkie, he couldn't help but lil-lady-fy her. On occasion Vicky helped him out with dust-ups, taking things down a notch, smiling, acting wise—which she was, always—and sweet, which she was, sometimes. On occasion, like now, she helped him get a read on a body.

I need you to do it fast, he told Vicky when she climbed into the Bug in her nurse's uniform. But do it good. I need to know if she was beaten.

The Neeyanderthal started shaking with laughter, stomach only. They both gaped at him.

The fuck did you have for breakfast, man? asked the Redeemer.

It's just, that's what I tell the ladies too: Gonna do you fast, but good.

No one else laughed. Seeing Vicky's look of hatred, the Neeyanderthal tried to put things right: Oh, hey, sorry bout the trucker mouth. It just slipped out.

If only you really were a trucker, Neeyan, Vicky said. But you're not, you're just tedious. The most tedious people in the world can't take anything seriously. Don't worry tho—and with this Vicky patted the Neeyanderthal's cheek—don't worry, I speak Hombre, so I know you're not actively trying to be a prick, you just have no control over your little bullshit organ.

The Redeemer didn't know if the Neeyanderthal and Vicky truly hated each other or simply had their own brand of love. He remembered something that had happened just after the brother's death. They'd been out boozing and he heard the Neeyanderthal recount the accident to a woman, the whole damn thing—stupid pedestrian, flipped truck, death throes—as a line. Neeyan didn't actually want to open up to the woman, but he recited the drama in an attempt to open up her blouse. The Redeemer had said to Vicky that that was low, even for the Neeyanderthal, but she put on a sad that's-not-the-whole-story face and said What do you expect, Neeyan cuts a profit whenever he can, and right now all he's got is his scar. If there was a market for it, he'd cultivate kidney stones and piss them out. Leave him be.

Before returning to Las Pericas they made a stop at Vicky's ex-boyfriend's parents' place. Actually he was an ex-lover, one Vicky loved for real, but his time was up and she hadn't backed down over the ultimatum. Vicky might be willing to suffer but suffering wasn't marital status, and his marriage was already on public record.

They're in a state of total hysteria, she said, packed in like sardines because the alarm went off while he was over there with his wife. Dropped in to pay back some money he owed and now they don't want to leave . . . seems someone's sick, and he convinced them to let me stop in and have a look.

He: the ex-lover. Vicky's face softened a bit at the mention.

Can I go with you? the Redeemer asked. Might be able to get something from the father—the nouveau always have the lowdown on each other's riche. Maybe he's been cooped up so long he's ready to wag his tongue. Plus he knows me, I've worked with guys close to him.

Vicky took out a pair of latex gloves and handed them to the Redeemer.

Don't touch anyone.

They rang the bell. A clipped argument could be heard coming from within. Go; No, let him go; Fine, I'll go; No, don't you go, mother; Oh, let her go; No, I'll go.

Ha, Vicky snorted. Their servant split so it looks like they'll have to learn how to turn a doorknob on their own.

It was He who answered. No mask. He smiled poignantly. A smile that said I'll always love you but my promises are in the pawnshop. He was a sad, handsome little devil. He looked at the Redeemer like an electrician who'd come when the lights weren't broken.

He's with me, Vicky said, and he knows your father.

They were all in a living room full of wood-and-red-velvet furniture—nostalgia for a finer form of pretense. An antique apiece and a drink apiece. The mother in the armchair, vodka on the rocks in hand, sloshed; the perverse twenty-year-old little brother at one end of the sofa, whisky on the rocks in hand, sloshed; the father in a high-back armchair, brandy and coke in hand, episcopally sloshed. You could sort of see that they were scared, but could more clearly see their ennui. We never know how much we actually hate one another, the Redeemer thought, until we're locked in a room together.

Which one's the patient? Vicky asked, eyeing the range of red-faced tremble-handed possibilities.

The ex-lover pointed to a door:

Her.

Vicky shot him a profoundly scornful stare, nodded and went to open the door. At the back of the room, sitting on a bed, a woman in a blue dress sat holding a teacup. She was wearing makeup but it couldn't hide the sneer of someone who swallowed bile every day as tho it were water. Vicky observed her from the doorway, the Redeemer from the living room. She took two steps in, put her hands on her hips, observed the woman a little longer, turned and closed the door.

There's nothing wrong with her.

You didn't even examine her, he said.

Stop rationing her booze, that's what she needs.

The silence that ensued would have been awkward in any other room, but in that one each member of the family merely clutched their drink a little tighter before sinking back into a slight stupor. The Redeemer sensed this was his moment. He approached the father and crouched down.

Remember me?

The man made an effort to wrestle his way out from the bottom of the bottle, finally found his pupils and focused on the Redeemer.

You once got some photos back for a friend of mine.

The Redeemer smiled.

Exactly. I'm dealing with something less serious now, but I need some information. You know who the Las Pericas house belongs to? Place no one's lived for years?

The man seesawed behind his eyeballs, forward and back, as he thought it out. Except for a hand faintly jiggling his ice, the rest of his body was still.

The Fonsecas, he said. Tied up in some legal mess, I think, but far as I know, it's theirs.

Yes, it's theirs, the mother interrupted from the depths of her vodka, for as much good as it does them.

Thassaway it is with those sorts of families. Now it was the perverse baby brother who spoke in a whiskified slur. Don't matter how many houses they buy, they only know how to live in crappy-ass shacks.

The Redeemer felt his fist wanting to bust the kid's nose, in part for that remark, but more because he wanted to bust the monster's nose regardless. This was the first time he'd seen him in the flesh, tho he knew what a class act this little shit was. He and some other silverspoon whose family had a funeral home had been caught snapping shots of each other with the bodies they were supposed to prepare: posing as if kissing or slapping the corpses, drawing moustaches on the dead, sticking hats on them. Then some other kid they'd showed the photos to started telling people and it was about to blow into a big scandal when the Redeemer stepped in and disappeared the pics. The funeral home kid got a slap on the wrist; the little shit, not even that.

One more thing, Vicky said to the whole family. In case this is spread by mosquitos I'd recommend you stop wearing perfume; they're attracted to it.

No one said a word, nor did anyone except the ex-lover make a move to stand when Vicky and the Redeemer headed for the door, but Vicky put up a hand in front of his face and said That's far enough.

Back in the car, the Neeyanderthal said Bet they offered you a drink in there—and me out here like a dumbfuck.

On the way to Las Pericas the Redeemer saw a corner flower-stand peeking out above the hunkered-down city and thought of Baby Girl, alone, injured, growing cold in that house, no one to talk to her. He stopped, said Wait for me, got out, and bought flowers. There were no Day-of-the-Dead marigolds but they had gillyflowers. Now that he thought about it, that stand never seemed to close, even on holidays or the darkest nights.

They arrived and the Redeemer got out to speak to the Unruly, but she didn't need convincing because she'd seen who-knows-what in Vicky's authoritative eyes, so all Vicky had to say was Don't worry, I'll be right back.

She even reached out to tuck a strand of hair back behind the Unruly's ear and tho she didn't smile, she didn't flinch either.

They stayed in the car and smoked while Vicky worked. The Unruly smoked, too, leaning up against the doorjamb. They finished one cigarette. Lit a second. Finished the second and lit a third and that was when she came out. Vicky gave the Unruly a pat on the back, which morphed into some sort of sororal squeeze; she leaned in a little more and whispered to her. Then headed for the car.

What'd you just say? asked the Neeyanderthal.

That we women need to look out for each other. No one else is going to do it for us.

What did she die of? asked the Redeemer.

This shit. Vicky waved vaguely at the world outside the car. But she must have gone days without treatment to die like that. By the way she held her hands you can tell she couldn't stand the pain in her joints, and from the blood in her mouth and nose it's clear the symptoms advanced to late-stage with no meds.

So was that why they had her locked up?

She hasn't been dead long, but that girl was sick for days before they got to her.

Did they do anything to her . . . after she died?

Vicky stared straight ahead a few seconds without saying a word. She looked tired.

They didn't fuck her, if that's what you're asking, but they did something. That shitbag Dolphin put her underwear on inside out.

He had no idea who from but knew at some point a message would arrive. And when it finally did, he realized right away who was running the show on the other side of the corpse.

What's up, Friend? Meet you on the corner over by Casa Castro.

There was only one person who called him Friend with a capital F: the Mennonite.

The two of them had met on a job they worked together, in a place a long way away from the place the Mennonite called home. They were going to pick up a body. The deceased was a family friend, which was why when the Redeemer arrived he found the man attempting to stitch up a finger.

No way am I handing him over like this, as if he was off to just anywhere.

The Mennonite was standing on the corner like a tree that had sprouted out of the sidewalk. These days he no longer wore the denim overalls and straw hat but the workboots and plaid shirt were still there. His red beard spilled out the sides of his facemask.

They hugged and the Redeemer asked:

So. What brings you way over here? You never used to leave your land.

Well, you know. Unhappy people aren't the problem. It's people taking their unhappy out on you.

I do know. Yeah.

The Mennonite had left the land of his kith and kin on his own, and had adapted to the world of those always in a rush—silence and simple toil replaced by engines and cement. But at least back there he'd had his people nearby. Now, not even that. Who knows whose toes he must have stepped on, why he had to strike out on another path. Still. It was time to get on with it.

What's the story? he gestured toward the Castro place.

Boy's in there, the Mennonite responded. They didn't touch him.

I'm going to have to ask him that myself.

Fraid that's going be a bitch, Friend.

The twist in the Mennonite's lips filled the gaps left by his words. There was no longer a Romeo to ask.

Fuckit, said the Redeemer. Same story on this side.

He tried to explain in a way that made it seem he understood more than he did: the Fonsecas hadn't killed Baby Girl, she'd died of the disease, and all the body needed was to be prettied up a bit.

The Mennonite nodded and took a deep breath and then said This is the truly fucked-up part. Wait for me here. He turned and walked back to the Castro house.

In the two minutes that went by before Baby Girl's father came out, it felt like the street contracted and began to throb. The Redeemer took out a smoke then thought better of it and put it back in the pack, glanced at the Castros' place and then turned the other way. He crossed his arms. Fuckit, he repeated.

He heard the Castros' metal door open then slam shut, and then panting, encumbered by sobbing, and steps approaching. He shot a quick sidelong look at the Bug and with an almost-imperceptible hand-pat signaled Stay put to Vicky and the Neeyanderthal.

When he felt him a half-step away, the Redeemer turned to face the man. Tho they knew each other, Baby Girl's father stared and stared and stared without recognizing him, and steadily with each passing second the man aged as the news inhabited his body, despite his attempt to resist it, his attempt to hold it at bay with rage. He slammed the Redeemer against the hood of the Bug and started shouting in his face.

Bring her to me! You bring her to me now! In one piece, you sonofabitch! You bring her to me safe and sound, right now!

The man was clenching his fists and trembling and still making up his mind whether to throttle the Redeemer. Then his boys flew out of the house, berserk. The older one wielded a club and the younger one a bat, itching to find something to justify their tunnel vision, their hatred. As soon as he saw them, the Neeyanderthal got out of the Bug, thumbs hooked through his beltloops; Vicky stepped out too, slower, eyeing them from her side of the car. One of the two must have made an impression on the brothers, who continued their approach, but slower now. The younger pointed his bat in the Redeemer's face.

The Mennonite held a hand up and said That's not the way, son.

The kid stared at the Redeemer, reluctant to let go of his rage, but then his father began to sob and both boys dropped their weapons to the ground and held him.

The Redeemer thought they'd do better to scratch the wound than bandage it: those who lose a child shouldn't be consoled; parents die to make room for their kids, not the other way around. He wasn't being cruel; he just felt that a gash that deep had to be respected, not swaddled over with cuddles.

Sir, said the Mennonite, Will you let the nurse-lady in? Just for a minute.

The man nodded without looking up.

We're going in too, the Neeyanderthal said.

The man nodded again. Okay let's go, he said, turning toward the metal door and heading off, eight hundred years older than when he'd come out it the other way.

In the Castros' living room hung a family coat of arms. The Castros had been noblemen and lords in some century or

205

other in some castle or other on the opposite side of the world—and there was the colorful coat of arms to prove it. They were different from the Fonsecas that way: the only things the Castros held on to from their poorer days were those they'd marshaled up from many generations back. On the walls of the Castros' living room, besides the coat of arms, there was nothing but photos of the boys in team uniforms and a diploma granted to Baby Girl for having finished her degree in psychology. Psychology. For fuck's sake.

They descended a freezing staircase. The basement was full of shadows cast by a dim corner lamp backlighting a dozen chains with hooks from which hung calves, turkeys, and half a cow. The Redeemer didn't say a word but at the sight of his raised brows, Castro said We don't trust outside meat.

In a room adjacent to their private abattoir he saw Romeo, laid out atop some boxes. One of his legs was falling off the side, as tho he'd made a quick move to get up. They encircled the body in silence. Only the Neeyanderthal rubbed his hands together, saying Damn it's cold. Vicky approached and began to study what was once Romeo. The Redeemer noticed he was dirty, that he still reeked of alcohol and had marks on his knuckles but no sign of blows to the face. Vicky examined his head and opened his shirt and palpated his ribs, sunken, beneath a blue bruise. The Redeemer turned to the Castro kids, whose hands were in their pockets.

What went down, muchachos?

The Castro kids were spitting images of their father, differing only by the quantity of hair on their heads and the way their flesh fought what was going on inside each of them. The older one jerked his shoulders up and down in a childish gesture and said We didn't do jack. I mean, we talked shit earlier on, but we didn't fight.

We liked him, said the younger one, sneaking a look at his father and continuing. Our jefe here always says the Fonsecas are fuckin users and climbers, but the son was a good kid.

So what'd you say? This was on Lover's Lane, right?

Mhm, said the older one. We saw him on our way into Metamorphosis, and since he was going somewhere else we thought he was headed for the swanky strip club, so my bro here said Hey, pretty boy, this ain't Vegas you know, and he said Fuckin deadbeats, I come here cos I carry big bills, not loose change. Stuff like that.

But we were just smacktalking, said the younger one. Even if it sounds like we wanted to fight.

There's some people you just mess with, that's just the way it is, said the older one.

The Redeemer nodded. He knew what they meant.

Then what?

That was early, the older one said. We took off after a little while to hit the other clubs, and we were on our way when we saw Romeo again, he was pretty looped, in the parking lot— no idea where he was going but he was staggering back and forth—and that was when he got hit by a van. It was backing up and I don't think they even saw him.

The Redeemer stiffened in shock but didn't dare turn and look at Vicky to corroborate what they were saying.

A van? You're telling me a vehicle did this to him?

S'right. Tapped him and took off. Me and my bro here went to see if he was okay. He wasn't breathing good but said not to call an ambulance, said it would pass. We picked him up and put him in the back seat of my car. Then we took off too, but on the way he asked us not to take him to the hospital, said please just let him hang with us a while, lay low and then he'd go home.

The Redeemer walked over to stare at the boys, straight into their eyes—back, forth, one, the other—searching for signs of a leaky lie.

And you didn't lay a hand on him. That was it. You're sure.

The boys nodded.

Well, said the older one, not all of it. We brought him back here and we were going to call a doctor but when we got him into the house he suddenly got real real light, and then heavy, and it took us a few minutes to realize he'd died since we didn't think he was doing that bad.

Here? Kid was sick and you brought him down here?

No, upstairs, we were in the living room. But then someone called.

A girl, the younger one piped in.

Yeah, a girl, and she said the Fonsecas had Baby Girl and weren't giving her back till we brought them Romeo. Which is why we didn't call and brought him down here instead, so he wouldn't rot.

The Redeemer turned to Romeo, whose hands Vicky was now examining. Romeo looked rough, but like his rough had come from earlier stuff and not from dying, as if the only thing dying had done was ashen up his skin, but you could tell there was prior pain.

Give us a minute, the Redeemer said, not turning to anyone in particular, and the Castros left the room.

By the way, the Mennonite said. Someone's out to jack you up. Boyfriend of one of your neighbors. Watch your ass, amigo.

Fuckit, how did little beau slick get word? And how did the Mennonite, who wasn't even from around here, know about it?

You giving me a tip-off or a warning? he asked.

Both, but not cos anybody told me to. Little punk's got no balls of his own and was looking for a hardcase to rough you up. Guy I know got asked and I'm just passing it along, free of charge.

The Redeemer shrugged no-big-thing shoulders and asked So, what about this?

The Mennonite crossed his arms and eyed Romeo.

I think they're telling the truth.

Not entirely, said Vicky. I buy the story about the truck but that doesn't explain his hands.

Oh, the Mennonite said. That was me.

The other two stared.

He looked a little too tidy to have died in a brawl.

He didn't die in a brawl.

But his father isn't going to believe that, is he? Why make matters worse by saying they didn't lay a hand on him? Those two families got bad blood between them. So let them believe what they want to believe, let them bury their boy like a hero. They're not going to simmer down when someone tells them to, they'll do it when they're worn out. So tell them what happened, but let him look like he had a fight first.

Vicky looked as if she was about to say something but thought better of it. And then she said: Why wouldn't he want to be taken to hospital?

Now that part I can't explain, the Mennonite replied.

They walked out and Romeo remained alone once more. They went upstairs to the Castros and before they left the mother appeared, frightened and pale, and demanded Now tell me what they did to my little girl.

The Redeemer decided the Mennonite's strategy wouldn't wash with her and said: More or less the same as what happened here. A tragedy with no one to blame.

What are you saying? That she's dead? That each of us ended up with the other's body by accident? Is that what you're telling me?

Something like that, yes.

The mother stared straight at him and said Those things just don't happen.

Some sad fuck so much as takes a bite of bread and we got to find a name for it, he thought. Or an alias anyway. That's about as close to the mark as we get.

Banished man alias Mennonite. Broken man alias Redeemer. Lonely old soul alias Light of my life. Ravaged woman alias Wonder where she's gone. Get revenge alias Get even. Truly fucked alias Not to worry. Contempt alias Nobody remembers him. Scared shitless alias Didn't see a thing. Scared shitless alias Doing just fine. Some sad fuck alias Chip off the old block. Just what I was hoping for alias You won't get away with this. Housebroken words alias Nothing but truth.

I got to buy condoms, the Redeemer remembered aloud.

Vicky eyed him mockingly.

What, your hands are too calloused?

No. From time to time there occurs a miracle.

Vicky gaped as if to say You got to be kidding—you, talking miracles? But Vicky didn't get it. Vicky was beautiful and a hardass and used to striding across a room and grabbing any man she wanted by the balls and dragging him into her bed without losing her head or getting quixotic. She'd never had to work to find someone to fuck, and he pitied her that a bit, just as he pitied those who don't know what it feels like to see a big city for the first time because they grew up in it, or the guy who can't recall what it is to feel handsome for the first time, or to kiss someone who seemed impossible to kiss for the first time. Vicky knows nothing of miracles.

Yeah, sometimes the ladies let their guard down, right? the Neeyanderthal said.

Oh god, said Vicky.

Here we go, she's going to tell me off.

No, I'm not, it's just that you don't get it. At all. See, men will fuck a chair, even if it's missing a leg, but when women fuck an ugly man or a jerk it's not because we'll fuck any old thing, it's cos that's the way things start and we know there's more to it. Men don't come to see that till years later, once they've stopped mounting anything that crosses their path.

Thanks, sweetheart, I knew one of these days you'd come to appreciate us.

This only applies to men with a soul, Neeyan.

So maybe Vicky simply understood different things. Either way, the Redeemer braked and left the two of them there in their silence when he caught sight of a pharmacy. He got out of the car but immediately saw it was closed, and the metal shutters had been beaten repeatedly with a pipe or a club or

211

a desperate fist, and beside the shutter hung a penciled sign reading *No facemasks.*

Dammit. Oh well, he had work to do. Maybe he'd find somewhere open on the way. He returned to the Bug and rolled down the window so as not to hear the silence between Vicky and Neeyan, but the silence of the street slipped in instead: a stubble field of frantic signals emitted from the antennae that fear had planted in people's heads. He could sense the agitation from behind their closed doors but sensed no urgent need to get out. It was terrifying how readily everyone had accepted enclosure.

He drove back to the Castro house, didn't stop, circled the block twice and headed for Las Pericas. He had to see where he'd hit a checkpoint, which he would: no such thing as a free ride, no matter how hard you hope. A block before Las Pericas they came upon another funeral procession. Normally he'd have passed it, to avoid waiting out the whole mournful motorcade, but this was the saddest cortege he'd ever seen: in the hearse no one but the chauffeur, and behind the hearse one lone Bug with a single person inside, facemasked.

He circled the block Las Pericas was on then headed to the Neeyanderthal's, assessing the street all the while. One would think he'd find fewer obstacles than ever, but the fear seeping from beneath people's doors threw him off his game; he stopped at every corner to look both ways, glanced in the rearview every twenty seconds, and each time he did he saw the same thing: asphalt about to rear up at him. Things had been roiling in the background for some time, but now you could see the bubbles starting to rise.

He dropped the Neeyanderthal at his place and the man got out without a goodbye for anyone. Next he headed for Vicky's. They passed the funeral procession once more, stopped now at a checkpoint. One soldier was opening the coffin and two more interrogated the chauffeur and lone mourner.

Assholes, said Vicky. As if the corpse is armed.

They passed one more pharmacy, also closed, with a sign in the window: *Closed for funeral.* He dropped Vicky at her place and made for his own. Perhaps he should do the swap there, given how riled up both families were. When he got back he saw that on the house next door someone had written on the wall *Clean up you pigs that's why we're in this shit.* And sure enough, there was a black puddle running from the front door to the gate, tho no insects hovered over it. He looked up. In truth there was nothing to see but a wall of tepid clouds blocking the stars.

He walked into the Big House. Standing a moment at one end of the hall he debated which of the four doors to head for: the anemic student's, to smack him around for being a shitstirrer; Three Times Blonde's, where he'd fall to his knees and beg Please please please, for the love of all good things, wait for me just a little longer; his own, to see what was going on; or la Ñora's, to sound her out about the body swap. Bingo.

He knocked. He heard no steps but la Ñora opened almost immediately, without looking through the peephole. She eyed the Redeemer with an odd intensity, trying to place him or perhaps keep him at bay. She said not a word.

Good afternoon, señora, said the Redeemer.

Evening, you mean, la Ñora replied automatically, tho it seemed like her mouth hadn't moved.

Right, yes, evening. Ahh, listen, señora, I just wanted to let you know I'll be having some people over tomorrow. Not for long—they'll just deliver something and go—but there will be several of them.

La Ñora stared, no change to her inscrutable expression.

I wanted to let you know so you don't worry, in case you hear anything.

You're going to have people over, la Ñora said. And you want me to keep my nose out of it.

Sharp lady, la Ñora.

The Redeemer smiled. Just don't want to worry you, señora.

La Ñora gave a nod. The Redeemer, too, nodded good night and turned. As he was about to enter his place la Ñora said Sir, then faltered. Young man, she tried again: have you seen the boy?

Answer me but keep your nose out of it, she said with her eyes. On the surface she looked the same as always, fierce and wary, but the Redeemer saw, now, a certain tender tremble and almost wanted to embrace her. He'd keep his nose out of it, tho. The anemic student. Who'd have thought.

No, he said. But I'll let you know if I do.

La Ñora nodded again and closed the door. The Redeemer stood a few seconds struggling with mental images of la Ñora and the anemic student, ate a two-day-old sweet roll and went to knock on Three Times Blonde's door. He heard her body stylizing its steps and saw the light behind the peephole go dark. They both stood breathing silently but the door didn't budge. Finally Three Times Blonde said Have you been wearing that facemask all day?

Yes, the Redeemer lied.

Three Times Blonde waited another minute and opened up slow. She took a step back, and the Redeemer walked in and shut the door. The moment he did, he cornered Three Times Blonde, pulled down his facemask and began to kiss her. She let him, arms at her sides, body limp but tongue responsive. In that single second the Redeemer thought of all the people who'd breathed in his face that day and the bug he'd smashed on his neck and the who-knows-what already coursing through his veins, yet here he was, a brazen bastard overexcited at the miracle of breasts and diereses before him. What a sonofabitch. Maybe she could sense the Redeemer's black dog pawing at her chest. Maybe she simply wanted to know. Either way Three Times Blonde pushed him aside.

So who you been talking to?

Lots of people.

Who you been talking to about me, you swine? she asked, and on stressing the *me* scratched the Redeemer's arm with a long red nail.

Not a soul. Why?

After you left my baby came over all keyed up wanting to yell at me, asking who'd I let in my house and I don't know what-all.

That wasn't me. That was the damn neighbor.

Three Times Blonde looked unsurprised.

I know.

So why ask?

Because men always talk. It's like they have to report everything to their friends. Jerks.

Ouch. Three Times Blonde had taken a shot in the dark and hit him right between the eyes. And called the other asshole baby.

He left without even saying goodbye, she continued, looking mournful. The Redeemer stroked her cheek.

You feeling sad? he asked, suave.

No.

Three Times Blonde slid her hand under his shirt and stroked his chest, then suddenly slid it down into his pants and squeezed his cock, palming his balls, weighing them.

The condoms, she said.

The Redeemer pulled her in by the back of the neck and began to kiss her. She tried to pull away and oh did he not want that to happen, please no, and in his head he attempted to shoo the bugs and people and shuttered pharmacies, but inevitably Three Times Blonde pulled his arm off her and scooted aside and said Pull . . . out . . . a . . . condom.

The Redeemer donned a now-where-did-I-put-it? face and for a second fostered hopeless fantasies of finding an open drugstore, but before he could lie again, Three Times Blonde said You didn't buy any. Stupidass neighbor. You didn't buy any.

She did stick-em-up hands, as tho she couldn't even bear to brush up against the Redeemer, opened the door, and said I got shit to do.

He begged and pleaded for a moment with his eyes and with her eyes she told him to go fuck himself, and so he went, pitiful and utterly dejected, and let the slam of the door push him home.

He walked in and threw himself down on the bed.

Some nights, when the black dog left, he imagined sleeping curled up inside some other animal, protected from the cold. But that night the black dog stayed.

216

4

In the faint light of his fitful sleep he saw Óscar's outstretched hand, pointing, and suddenly sat up in bed because he knew somehow it contained a clue to how this grimreapery had begun. He called the Mennonite, explained what he was thinking and they agreed to meet on Lover's Lane. Back to the Bug he went, back to streets buzzing behind closed doors, back to zigzagging around corners rife with aimed rifles, rife with thugs both uniformed and civilian. When he arrived the Mennonite was already waiting at the entrance to Metamorphosis. There were lights all down the lane and cars outside the cathouses but no one wandering from one to the next. They walked into Metamorphosis and he scanned the bodies below in search of Óscar.

The place was packed, placid but packed. There were people asleep underneath tables and asleep on top of tables—like really sleeping, not booze-induced sleeping. And those who were awake were conversing with the dancers. Normally they paid little attention, as if women taking off their clothes before a gaggle of drunkaneers was totally unremarkable; now they sat, chatting, nobody drooling, nobody tail-shaking. One lonely soak at the bar slurred It's aaaaaaaall over, It's aaaaaaaall over, again and again and again. Everyone else was cool and attentive, as if listening to hailstones on a tin roof.

They haven't been out for days, he heard Óscar say behind him. Claim it's too dangerous but you ask me, this is their chance of a lifetime.

I see you made use of those facemasks, the Redeemer said. One girl was dancing before a cluster of liquored-up fools, naked but for the mask over her mouth; each time she leaned close she made as if to take it off, and the boozers whooped in titillation.

Fuck yeah, said Óscar.

Óscar, the Redeemer said. The Fonseca kid. You sure bout where you saw him come out of?

Óscar glanced at him for a single second: long enough to draw up, read through, sign and notarize a confidentiality clause between the two of them.

Girls' place, yeah, he said. He was referring not to these girls, the working girls, but to the customers.

Appreciate it, brother.

They left Metamorphosis and entered Incubus. The clientele was less numerous but more boisterous, only a dozen or so women, rorty and sloshed. They sat at the tables with two or three strippers, drinking. The floor was empty.

The Mennonite addressed the madam, a stout elegant woman with very black hair.

I'm looking for a boy.

Hm. We generally cater to a female clientele but it's always possible to arrange something.

The Mennonite cast a glance around the tomcathouse, studying the handful of men, and said: I'm looking for one with a steady boyfriend.

The madam observed them distrustfully. Then she got it.

Must be that one, and she pointed to a young man, almost a teenager really, attempting to smile at the woman buying him drinks. He's been acting all mopey. Must've had a fight with his boyfriend; guy used to come pick him up after work but I didn't see him last night.

They approached the table where he sat. The Redeemer bent over the woman the kid was hooking until he was almost brushing her cheek.

Let me borrow him for one sec, amiga, just a quick word and then he's all yours.

She batted her eyes diplomatically and the Mennonite nodded the boy over to the next table.

I don't sleep with men, he said as soon as they sat down.

We know, said the Mennonite. Or rather, you only sleep with one.

The Mennonite spat the words, resting his hands on the table as if he might backhand the boy at any moment. The kid suddenly looked scared. The Redeemer's approach was more gentle.

Tell us what happened two nights ago.

He came in. We argued about the same thing as always— and with this he gestured, taking in the whole of the whorehouse with one hand—then he took off. Didn't even wait for his sister.

His sister. Fuckit.

Did they come together?

Yeah, but he ran off and it took her a minute to follow. It was crowded that night. And then neither of them came back.

They rose, intending to leave, but the boy stopped the Redeemer with an arm. What is it, what happened to him?

Get some sleep, the Redeemer said. But tell them to give you the day off tomorrow. By then we'll know for sure.

They walked out and the Redeemer lit a cigarette and stood smoking by the Bug. It was time to call Dolphin. He dialed.

I got bad news, he said.

Dolphin was silent, or his mouth was anyway; the lung wheezed.

Romeo's dead, he said. But the Castros aren't to blame.

He listened to Dolphin wheeze down the line and then hang up with no reply.

He was tired of delivering that kind of news, and now he felt bad for not having delivered it to the one person who may have truly cared. Motherfuckit.

He got a very few hours of straggly shuteye, alternating between simple dreams of tires in motion and cats on ledges, and got up with neither vigor nor languor. Please let it be a dull day and not some deranged vigil.

He tried Gustavo again, the know-it-all legal beagle. Not home. Letting himself be guided by an early morning urge he got back in the Bug and drove around behind the Big House for a tamale sandwich; only at the empty corner did he remember there was no one out on the streets. He was hungry as hell. And thirsty. But all there was was rankys-tank water in a few puddles on the path and those dense gray clouds that refused to squeeze out a drop. A synthetic insanity to the weather, the city, the people, all sulking, all plotting who-knows-what.

He headed for Las Pericas. Suddenly he saw something in the middle of the street and slammed on the brakes. A huge heap of rags, or hacked-up dogs. He dodged the pile and eyed it as he passed: it was neither of those things; it was a man, black with sludge. The Redeemer thought he looked familiar. He rolled down the window and stuck his head out. It was the junkman he'd come across the day before, mouth stuffed full of facemasks, eyes wide as an illuminati. The Redeemer rolled up the window, rolled on.

Before ringing the bell at Las Pericas he pulled the facemask out of his pocket. It was stiff with too much spit on one side, too much world on the other; what good was that now? He put it back in his pocket and rang the bell.

The Unruly poked her head out a window, then opened the door and stood to one side. The Redeemer walked in and saw they'd put several bags of ice on Baby Girl, whole unopened bags. Despite all the ice it was as if you could see new life there, see some color, sense something new inhabiting her. He pulled off the bags and tossed them aside. Then he tried to lift her, but she was so heavy. He looked at the Unruly, maybe she'd agree to help, she seemed softer, more compliant than before; but in the end he decided to carry the body by himself. We're going to be all right, he said to the shell of Baby Girl as he hoisted her up in his arms and headed out into the leaden morning.

The Unruly, without his asking, walked alongside, opened the Bug's door and even shifted the passenger seat up so he could place her inside. Her body wasn't yet stiff, so he was able to arrange it as tho Baby Girl had curled up for a siesta on a road trip, raising her head from time to time to ask Are we there yet, are we there yet?

.   .   .

What's this? Where to? asked the Redeemer as he watched the Unruly get in as well.

I'm coming with you.

Didn't they tell you how this works? Me and another guy like me make sure everything's okay, and then—and only then—do we make the switch.

Right. But they also told me to see where you put her. It's not like you're the one running the show.

He started the car. No sooner had he turned the corner than he saw a couple kids take off running, something in their arms. He had a hunch what it was about and pulled up. Indeed, someone had broken the lock on a corner store and they were looting the place bit by bit. Lowlifes. Still, he stopped the car, got out, grabbed a few bottles of water and two prepackaged sandwiches, and left a few bills on a high shelf in the hopes that the kids wouldn't be able to reach them. He was wolfing down the sandwiches before he'd even left the store.

There were even fewer cars out now. On one avenue, where trying to cross normally meant taking your life in your hands, the only thing on the street was the fear of penned-up people. As if everyone's prejudices about everyone else had suddenly been confirmed.

They say some people are spreading it on purpose, the Unruly announced, as tho they'd both been thinking the same thing.

He didn't reply but did turn to look at her. He glanced at her hands: fleshy and soft, a yellowy stain at her fingertips. With all the facemasks he now looked more at eyes and hands. If this carried on, people would end up IDing one another by their fingernails.

I met your brother-in-law, he announced abruptly. The Unruly turned to him, little-girl fear on her face.

That's right, the Redeemer said. You going to tell me what happened?

The Unruly stared straight ahead and crossed her hands, struggling for self-possession. The Redeemer decided to push a little harder.

Romeo. The Castros didn't touch him, did they.

The Unruly shook her head slowly side to side.

No. When I went outside he was already on the ground and they were just going to him.

And why didn't you go to him too?

Now it was her turn to stare at her hands or perhaps out past her hands.

The Redeemer was about to ask something else but she said: He didn't like for people to see him sad, down. I don't know if that was why—because he'd have hated me for seeing him like that—or if I was too drunk to understand what was going on. I'm drunk almost all the time.

This girl would cry if she had any fucking idea how, thought the Redeemer, seeing the way she let her eyes fall to the floor, utterly defeated. And then the Unruly did cry, cried short and hard, without changing her expression, maybe without realizing she was crying.

He didn't want to go out, he really didn't, she repeated. He was scared of this shit. The sick people, all those dirt-bags coughing up blood. He didn't even like going to the doctor, he was that scared of places with so many fucking sick people.

So why'd you snatch Baby Girl?

My father said to, told us to take one of the Castros, said this time they were going to pay, is what he said. So I went out because I'd seen Baby Girl hanging around here before and she was always alone. When I found her she was leaving home, on her way out, and she looked bad; I told her to come with me and she didn't even ask why or where to. When I got her home my father was so happy, and then we put her in the car and took her to Las Pericas. That's when I saw she had blood coming out her mouth. We put her to bed but she didn't last long after that.

But didn't you ask Dolphin why he was doing it?

I did, but all he said was: Be loyal to your family, do as I say. So I said I'm sure Romeo isn't that bad off. I don't know if he really believed me or whatever it is he has against the Castros just became more important, but the only thing he said was: He's my son, I'll handle it how I see fit.

The things people inscribe on tombstones, even if only with their breath. I will love you always. I can never forgive you. Forget about me. I'll be back. You'll pay for this. Words that etch deeper than a chisel. Erasing those things was what the Redeemer was there for. He excelled at nothing but the ability to diminish malediction; to free folks from cell blocks, or their own promises. The fact that he was never in the way meant he could be used like a screwdriver and then stuck back in the toolbox, no need to thank him at all. That fix you're in? Take care of it *entre nous*. That secret of yours? We'll keep it *entre nous*. That fine you got? *Entre nous*, let's lower it; that alibi you need, *entre nous* we'll cook it up. Dirtywork is providence.

That was what he knew, how to efface set-in-stone truths. But he still had nothing to grab hold of in this tale of lonely deaths, nothing but pieces of lies. Solid lies, but lies nonetheless.

In the rearview he saw a black truck riding up on them hard, several yards behind. He slowed to let them pass but the truck pulled alongside, someone in it looked at Baby Girl and then it cut them off. Two badasses emerged with faces that confirmed they were indeed very big badasses. The one who got out on the passenger side didn't have to tell the Redeemer to hustle. The Redeemer turned off the engine and got out. The badasses weren't wearing facemasks either.

Girl gets out too, said one of them.

The city had seen other times when people died by the cartload, but back then it was bankrolled black lung and mass mine collapses—the usual. Perhaps because life was short, people had learned not to stick their noses into the affairs of others: existence was already a bitch without worrying about them as well. Perhaps that was also why they were all so fixated on form, on nicedaying and areyouwelling and thankgodding and tookinding. Mechanisms to mark distance. But these thugs knew nothing of etiquette.

The Unruly got out of the car and went and stood behind the Redeemer, arms crossed.

What'd you do to the other girl? asked one.

Nothing, she died of this shit.

The badass adjusted his dark glasses, took a few steps toward the Bug, stared at Baby Girl a few seconds and returned.

You need the body?

I do, said the Redeemer. Only reason I'm out is so I can deliver it.

Thing is, we need a body, the badass said. But I guess there's lots of them around these days.

He said something to the other badass and they got back in their vehicle. The Redeemer and the Unruly returned to theirs.

Normally it's the dead that are rotten, not the living, the Unruly said.

Her proclamation made the Redeemer want to up and forget about everything and have everybody up and forget about him. He wanted to crawl under a rock or onto some furniture. Who knows why we were left here like collateral, he thought. I guess some other Redeemer will negotiate our release.

They arrived at the Big House and he handed the Unruly the keys to start clearing the way, got Baby Girl inside, lay her on his bed. The Unruly stared at the Redeemer's possessions as tho shocked to see he didn't live in a cave, then said I'm outta here, don't move her without telling us.

And she left.

The Redeemer leaned back against the wooden table by the bed and tried to look Baby Girl over with a professional eye, but it was hard since what he really wanted was to sit and hold her hand. So that was what he did. She was cold but still a little soft.

We'll get you cleaned up, young lady, he said.

He stood, smoothed her skirt, closed her eyelids all the way, combed her eyebrows. He found an iron he hadn't used in months, carefully removed Baby Girl's cardigan and ironed it on the table and then put it back on.

What else? He knew there was more but he had no desire to do those things and didn't know how. He'd ask Vicky to help. He pulled out his cell: no signal.

He went out to the street, arranged to go pick up Vicky, then called the Neeyanderthal. Get over here, it's almost time.

The Redeemer was about to go back into the Big House when he saw Three Times Blonde turn the corner. He stood waiting for her at the entrance and, when she arrived, gestured with his hands to say Huh?

Three Times Blonde tossed her head and said Seeing as you're so useless . . .

She took him by the hand and pulled him indoors. She walked in front, smiling at him—this time most definitely at him—with her little pantyline.

Before going into her place the Redeemer said Let me lock up.

Like you have treasure in there, she said, not knowing that today more than any other day he would have happily stabbed someone to protect what was inside.

He turned the key in his lock and went to Three Times Blonde's place; she took him to her room and pointed to the bed. Lie down.

The Redeemer lay down and in the time it took him to wriggle out of his clothes she'd taken off all hers. That was the first time he'd seen every bit of her, a burning miracle of flesh. He thought he might come just from staring at her waxed lips, her landing strip; that he might come in the anticipation of sucking her breasts, which looked larger and more obliging than last time; that he might come just from envisioning the feel of her ass in his hands and the way he'd lay her down on the bed and this time, yes, o thank you most holy saint of horndogs, finally they would fuck; and he tried to get up but she said No: I said lie down!

He lay down and watched Three Times Blonde touch herself with both hands; then she knelt on the bed and slid him into her mouth.

The Redeemer clutched at the sides of the mattress as she ran her mouth and hands over his cock. He wanted to say Stop, but never ever ever ever would he tell her to stop, and just in time she pulled him out and said There. She opened the little box of condoms she'd placed on the dresser and as she took one out the Redeemer said Weren't you scared of going out on the street?

What scares me is the stupid shit people are doing on the street. Not being there.

And she put the condom on him.

Don't do a thing, she said.

She knelt over the Redeemer and began very slowly to lower herself down so that he entered her. He could feel his cock changing temperature as it made its way inside. Three Times Blonde began moving in circles, moving almost without moving, from the inside out. Then she let herself fall over him, brushing his chest with her nipples, and slipped her tongue into his mouth, and he ran his hands down her back and held her hips, which never stopped grinding. Everything was better. She was better, life was better, this woman wetting herself with his cock—nothing better could possibly occur in the rest of his everloving life. He made no attempt to show her what he could have done, and she fucked him at her own sweet speed, all by herself, until she straightened back up and came as if her bones were going to burst through her skin, arms back, stuttering one single vowel with each spasm. Then she fell back on top of him and he rocked her hips with his hands, and she continued to come in little splinters, in quick intakes of breath, until he too was done.

What colors did you see? he asked.

Black, she said.

He heard noise outside. His other instincts activated immediately; he moved Three Times Blonde gently, got up, put on pants and shirt, and left.

Dolphin was inside the Big House. He was bent over the Redeemer's door trying to work the lock with a credit card. By his side, the Unruly looked on anxiously.

What's wrong, Chief? the Redeemer asked.

Dolphin turned, looked the Redeemer over from head to bare feet, and said You didn't tell me you were bringing her over here already. Didn't even give me a chance to leave her a little token of appreciation. You go on back to whatever you're up to, don't mind me.

Fraid you can't do that, Chief.

Dolphin straightened up with difficulty and gazed into the Redeemer's eyes.

Trust me, kid, I got your back.

And lightly palmed his cheek several times, pat pat pat.

The Redeemer sensed his black dog there behind the door, silent, hulking, like the very first time he appeared, when Dolphin had said exactly the same thing, years back.

He wasn't the Redeemer back then; back then he was nothing but a brickshitting ambulance-chaser carving out a career in fifth-rate courts.

Some buzzmen had stopped by the pen to beat the ever-loving life out of a man who was already all bloodied up, a mess of a man kicked more times than he could take. Don't let him get away, they'd said on their way out, as if the man could do anything but cower in a corner and swell up.

The man was fading in and out and on one of the ins stared back with his single working and seriously crapkicked eye. It was an empty stare, pure light in a pure state, until he managed to force all his strength into it and said something, his pupil dilating. Help me, or Don't leave me alone, or Touch me, or Release me. He approached the man, who made slow mysterious gesticulations in the air. What, what, what do you want me to do? The man kept his good eye glued on him, and it slowly shrank smaller and smaller then opened wide one last time along with his one last breath and he couldn't even take the man's hand, so he crouched down before his face, not voicing a word but with his eyes saying Hold on, hold on, we'll work it out.

A few minutes later the buzzmen were back, and wordlessly one grabbed the man by the armpits and the other by the ankles and they began to lift. That was when the Redeemer came to life and, in an authoritative stance he was only just learning, stood blocking the cell door and said Hold on now, hold on, we still have to issue the paperwork. The buzzmen glanced at him and took no notice, as tho he were a frail little boy talking to his stuffed animals. They went back to what they were doing and he said No! I said no! We haven't contacted his next of kin! He'd raised his voice but beneath the words could be heard the start of a sob. This time, for the first time, the buzzmen stared at him with faces that said The fuck does this little shit think he's doing? and put the body down—a body they knew was not the kind of body you take to the family—and stood clenching and unclenching fists, reconciled to a whole other asskicking, but suddenly it was not their fists but someone else's hand he felt on his shoulder, and he turned and saw the biggest bastard in the barrio, the one who'd gotten him this gig, who said: Thanks for everything, counselor, we'll take it from here. And the big bastard smiled at him like a brother.

He thought of the man's look, which he'd never gotten out of his head; of what he himself looked like in the other man's eyes; of the fact that some sort of agreement had been reached in that final moment, when he shook his head mechanically side to side, more an entreaty than an order.

The barrio bastard, who at the time had a whole nose and both lungs, gestured affably to the buzzmen to take the body out as tho waving them into his house, then faced him and said it: Trust me, kid, I got your back.

And he decided not to keep shaking his head, not to keep blocking their way with his own body to prevent them from removing the other, not to say a word. And that was the precise instant when he first felt the presence of the black dog, who would never again leave him, who might sometimes slip out of sight, but would always be there.

He learned to live with the cur, at times even to conjure him. Yes, something inside him broke, but that's what made it possible to go places and make decisions he could never have stomached on his own. His black dog was a dark mass that allowed him to do certain things, to not feel certain things, he was physical, as real as a bone you don't know you have until it's almost jutting through your skin.

The Redeemer recalled all of this and brought his face up close to Dolphin's and said again, nearly touching his nose, Fraid you can't do that.

Dolphin pulled back a bit and eyed him with scorn.

Why's that? Because you got your little door locked?

So the Redeemer pulled out his key, slipped it in the lock, turned it, opened the door and stood aside.

Still can't do that.

Dolphin, face still full of scorn, said You'd drown in a glass of water, and placed a hand on the doorjamb, but at that moment the Unruly grabbed him by one wrist.

The man said no.

Dolphin turned to her in utter astonishment. There had to be some mistake.

We can talk later, now stop fucking around and behave.

But jerking his arm, the Unruly spun him around.

No. It's time for you to grit your teeth and swallow.

Dolphin was about to say something but she squeezed his wrist a little tighter.

Enough. Don't be stupid.

Dolphin glanced down at the arm cuffed by his own daughter's hand for a few seconds, perhaps listening to himself wheeze, then nodded as tho he'd been the one who decided to go. He cast the Redeemer a casual sidelong glance by way of farewell and ambled slowly toward the entrance.

At the door he turned for a moment and said One of these days something terrible is going to happen.

And left.

That it might, the Redeemer thought, But no way am I letting you in to despoil a dead body.

Before going back inside Three Times Blonde's he went to the Big House door to make sure it was actually locked but first stepped out on the street. Still an overcast morning, he thought. Afternoon, he corrected himself. We're still alone, not even anyone to offer wrong directions. And then he thought he heard a muffled sound to his left, but didn't bother to turn and look to see what it was, since nothing but the lingering trace of silent complaint seemed possible in that bleak and stricken city. Or because his black dog wasn't there to remind him that anything was possible. And he felt a cold wooden crack! on his cranium and saw the sidewalk rush up at his face and then took the tip of a shoe to his ribs and then to his cheekbone and a heel rammed repeatedly into his ear. It hurt like a bitch, he had to start hitting back, beat the motherloving life out of someone, he said to himself, and still hoped he might as he clamped onto a fist that he used to raise himself, but then came another blow and something in him disconnected, like he'd been detached from a rock and was falling through an open pit, dark and icy, a pit with no walls and no end.

5

He awoke and saw the overcast sky falling onto his eyes. It felt as tho the darkness had gone on for hours, but it couldn't have been more than a few minutes, since there was the Neeyanderthal, who'd said on the phone he was on his way over.

He'd dreamed. Or more than dreams he'd seen snapshots of a devious Egyptian bug clamping gleefully onto his neck.

It looked like a block party, with all the people there outside the Big House: a white-shirted, blue-trousered buzz-cut heap of a man lay sprawled a few inches away; the Neeyanderthal stood effortlessly restraining Three Times Blonde's slicked-back jack on the ground; and Three Times Blonde herself was peering from the half-open door of the Big House, her face fearful but also sort of fascinated.

No, really, it's all over, here, let me help you up, Neeyan was saying to the guy. Let me give you a hand.

The little jack made as if to accept the offer and the Neeyanderthal pushed him back down, all the force of his open hand on the man's face.

Don't raise your hand to me, you little shit.

And he laughed and said No no, sorry brother, I was being a dick, here, get up, we'll talk.

Little slick conched himself into his tiny shell of a world there on the sidewalk and the Neeyanderthal smacked him again.

Answer when you're spoken to.

Enough, Neeyan, the Redeemer said from his own piece of sidewalk. It's not like the little prick doesn't have motive.

We're just having a chat, the Neeyanderthal replied.

The Redeemer himself had been shitkicked in seconds, so who knows how the Neeyanderthal had managed to take the two of them down with no help from anyone. Maybe he should feel guilty for mixing his friend up in fights that weren't even his, but some time ago he'd decided that if the man wanted to kill himself anyway, why worry about it. I am one lowly sonofabitch, he thought.

From the corner of his eye he glimpsed something stirring, but by the time he turned to look, the heap that had accompanied little slick was already on his feet and wielding a blade with the resolve of a man who doesn't carry it for effect. He lunged at the Neeyanderthal, who for a split second made no move, his face saying Whatever shall be shall be—like this was some sort of favor—and when the tip of the blade was almost to his stomach he snatched the heap's wrist with one hand and twisted, but the rest of the body failed to turn at the same speed and you could clearly hear how his wrist went snap before the whole heap of him slammed against the sidewalk.

The Neeyanderthal looked happy, as tho just bathed, or even born.

Maybe it's not that he wants to die, the Redeemer thought, but that what he wants is not to stumble.

Damn, Neeyan, he said, We ought to get you on TV.

Nah, the Neeyanderthal replied. No point being famous; then they'd just say I never existed.

The Redeemer got to his feet and said to the two bruisers: Go.

The heap crawled a few feet, then pulled himself up and quickly scampered to the corner. Little slick sat still in his own world, exploring the insides of his arms. Finally he stood and went to the Big House door. On seeing him Three Times Blonde slammed it shut.

You think you're coming in here? Look at you!

What?

There's an epidemic out there and you got nothing on. I bet you're already sick.

I had a mask on, whined her beau. But that bastard smacked it off.

There ensued a brief silence. Three Times Blonde cracked the door for a sec and stared him in the eye.

That's what they all say, she said.

And closed it again.

The minute Not-so-slick took his leave, Vicky turned up. She saw them all in the distance, standing before the Big House, and surveyed the terrain on approach. Before saying a word she followed him with her eyes, then looked at the Neeyanderthal, then at the bloody splash-up on the sidewalk, and finally at the Redeemer.

Want me to tell you about it? asked the Neeyanderthal.

Vicky scanned the scene again with something like a surplus of sadness and began to examine the Redeemer, feeling his neck, looking at his eyes, the cut above one brow, the split lip. The Redeemer's ribs were still shaking but she didn't think they were broken.

Open your mouth, Vicky said. The Redeemer opened his mouth and Vicky prodded a canine with one finger.

This tooth's done for, she said. But the rest of the prick'll survive.

One more thing, said the Redeemer: Check and see if I have anything here.

He pointed to his neck. Vicky tilted his head a bit and looked. She stood back, looked at him again.

What do you think you have there?

You see a welt?

Vicky looked again.

I see something, but it could be a heel mark. If you were going to die you'd feel awful by now. That's what I've been seeing at the hospital. Things don't usually escalate this quick, but sometimes these fuckers can remember if they've been in a certain place before, and that makes them really hard to stop. Things do more damage the second time around.

If it was merely a question of feeling awful, the Redeemer was infected as shit, but for now he felt the contamination was contained to the places he'd been kicked.

Let's go look at Baby Girl, he said.

I'm staying here, the Neeyanderthal said. More fun.

He opened the door and at that moment a call came in. Vicky went ahead.

Friend—it was the Mennonite—all good over there?

All good, why?

Just got word the Las Pericas place is on fire.

What the . . . ? he thought. How would the Mennonite even know to associate Las Pericas with Dolphin?

The place is on fire . . . And you're telling me the Castros aren't behind it, the Redeemer said.

I'm saying the Castros aren't behind it, the Mennonite

replied. Been here the whole time. All the father wants is his daughter back, and at a time like this his boys aren't about to do anything without his say-so.

Got it. All good here. Anything happens I'll give you a call.

They hung up. It was time to try Gustavo again. He dialed and found him in. Come on over, the man said.

He walked into the Big House. Inside his apartment, Vicky was washing one of Baby Girl's arms with a wet rag. Some bodies need to be assessed; this one needed to be dressed.

I'm leaving you here with her, he said. Won't be long.

Vicky nodded without turning to look, and the Redeemer walked out.

Be right back, he said to the Neeyanderthal.

Where you off to?

Going to see Gustavo, but I need you to stay here.

Bet you'll smoke a blunt, the Neeyanderthal said.

The Redeemer got into the Bug and drove off. On the way to Gustavo's he stopped a second in front of Las Pericas. The facade was still standing but the flames inside the place were devouring it all and already licking at the windows. No firemen or onlookers to distract the fire.

He got to Gustavo's. His was not a hood but a neighborhood, a bit better painted but equally as deserted as where the Redeemer lived. He got out, knocked and after a few seconds a girl came to the door. She couldn't have been more than fifteen or sixteen, and was pregnant. Come in, she said quietly, and turned.

The floors, walls, furniture, doorknobs, all of it possessed a soap-scrubbed shine, less a clean house than some sort of mausoleum holding the outside world at bay. Gustavo was sitting in an armchair in the living room. You could tell he'd just come from court because he'd yet to take off his coat and tie. The Redeemer hadn't laid eyes on him for a couple years. The man was still in shape, but his chin-sag and dark-circled eyes said he'd seen the better side of sixty some time ago. The girl handed the Redeemer a facemask. She looked sleep-deprived or anemic.

Mamacita, bring the attorney here a beer, Gustavo said.

On his way in, the Redeemer had not noticed that behind her was a boy with a baby-walker. Something was the matter with him. He was smiling and moving his legs but not making much progress, his eyes unfocused.

So, you working too?

Fraid so.

At the foot of the sofa sat a metal pail of marijuana. Gustavo took out a sheet of rice paper, then another, and licked the length of both to make one long sheet. He rolled a leisurely spliff as fat as a churro and when he saw the Redeemer eyeing it said I'm not giving you any; feel free to roll your own.

And toed the pail over to him.

I'm good, said the Redeemer.

So. How can I be of service?

The Las Pericas place.

What about it?

It's on fire.

Gustavo arched his eyebrows and opened his eyes wide but didn't release the tank of smoke he'd sucked into his lungs. He held it a few more seconds and then, after exhaling, said: God's will that was, I'm surprised it didn't happen sooner.

Why?

Had it coming, that's why.

Gustavo took another big hit of his spliff and waited, making the Redeemer work for it.

What happened?

They aren't two families is what happened, he replied: They're one, or almost, his voice tight with smoke. The two fathers have the same father. That's what happened.

And he expelled the smoke.

The Castros' father married on the up-and-up, but one day he got the hots for this girl in the neighborhood, took off with her and started another family. All well and good so far, right? Just the way it is. But then the old fucker went and died, fifteen years or so after he and his second woman had been living together. And that's when this all started up.

The girl came in with a beer for the Redeemer and Gustavo said Wait.

He stroked her ass and blew her a big smacking kiss. The girl remained motionless.

You'd never met my wife, had you? She's a saint. Okay, mamacita, now run and make me one of those highballs you're so good at.

The girl left.

Gustavo—this Gustavo—could never have existed in another age. For the first time in the history of humankind, legions of men his age could fuck like they were decades younger. The things they'll never discover, these old men who can still get it up, thought the Redeemer. As if there's nothing to be learned from defeat.

We live in extraordinary times, Gustavo said. People now-adays are aware of so much stuff going on in the world that they can handpick their memories. Didn't used to be like that, people used to live in whatever world their parents had left them. Some still do, like this gang—holding on and holding on.

To what?

The body. The day of the wake, the other family—the first one—came out, just to pay their respects and say their goodbyes. The widows greeted each another, the boys ignored each other—each family had a teenager almost the same age, see—and that was it. But when the Castros found out they were going to bury him who-knows-where, well that was the fuckin end of good form. Turns out the Fonsecas belong to some sort of sect, call themselves Christians but don't belong to the church.

It's always the other guy's religion that's a sect, isn't it? the Redeemer asked, unwisely, since he knew it was best to let people talk without rankling. Gustavo gave him a quick look like he'd had food thrown in his face, took another toke and continued.

After that, no surprises: widow number one asked them nicely not to bury him there, then demanded they not bury him there, but since the other one kept saying no no no, widow one said she wasn't going to let them do that, she wasn't the legitimate wife for nothing, they'd see. Off she went, lawyered up, and came back. The Fonseca widow said they better not think they were going to take the body, and the lawyers brought some cops along.

Did they get it?

Well sure—corpse was in their name. Son of the second family didn't even get his dad's last name, supposedly to avoid complications. Ha! So they kicked up a fuss, there was back-and-forthing, there were threats, but what I remember best is that kid, Dolphin. Back then he wasn't called that. The way he clenched his fists and stared at the coffin as they carried it out, his eyes little slits full of rage.

Gustavo leaned forward to check if his drink was on the way but couldn't see the kitchen from where he sat. The Redeemer could, tho, and saw the girl uncorking a bottle of brandy.

Thing is, he hadn't left a will, Gustavo continued, And the house where he and his second lady lived was in both their names, but the house they were about to move to was only in his.

Las Pericas.

Right. And ever since then there've been legal proceedings to see who gets to keep it, tho I know Dolphin has a key and pokes his head in, time to time. Might just be a good thing it's burning down. Nobody likes to share money, but it's easier than sharing a fistful of ashes.

They'd had no Redeemer to lend them a hand, the Redeemer thought.

Well now there's fewer to share them between, but more ashes to go around.

Eh?

Dolphin's son died, and so did the Castros' daughter. And each family has the other one's corpse.

For a second Gustavo's eyes popped out of their sockets.

Shoot-out?

Now the Redeemer was the one to enjoy letting the information steep a few seconds, as he took a sip of his beer.

Coincidence.

Gustavo narrowed his eyes.

Those things just don't happen, he said.

He was tempted to smoke a joint but decided not to ask. It was time to go. He glanced toward the kitchen to say goodbye to the girl and saw her with one hand inside Gustavo's glass, staring fixedly at the wall while she fingered the ice, as if cleaning it. The scene had the innocence of all unsettling things that take place in silence.

He bought more flowers on his way back and stopped to watch a madman who used to bounce around among the cars until one of them would whack him to the curb. Now, with no traffic, he was walking on the sidewalk.

What you doing? he asked. But the madman only stared as tho the question was idiotic.

He arranged with the Mennonite to make the trade on the corner closest to the Big House. With the way the city was, better to do it quick and out in the open than try to find some other spot. He called Dolphin, too, and told him it was time, that he should head over, but to let him do his job.

The Neeyanderthal had gone inside and was sitting in his apartment having coffee with Vicky, next to the bed where Baby Girl lay. The water must've come back on.

They're on the way, he said. Look alive, Neeyan, and let me know when they get here.

The Neeyanderthal finished his coffee and left. The Redeemer took his seat.

I won't mix you up in this shit again, he told Vicky.

At least this time it feels like it matters, she replied.

They said nothing more. Everything was so quiet you could hear Baby Girl's silence, as tho she'd absorbed every sound in the room. It was hard and yet formless, that silence. How to describe what isn't there? What name can you give to something that doesn't exist yet exists for that reason precisely? Kings of the kingpins, those who had invented the zero, he thought, had given it a name and even slipped it into a line of numbers, as tho it could stay put, obedient. But once in a while, like at that moment, there before Baby Girl, zero rose up and swallowed everything.

They're on the corner, the Neeyanderthal shouted from out front.

I'll get Neeyan so he can help you carry Baby Girl, Vicky said.

No no no, that cat's too rough, he might hurt her.

Vicky stood and stared, in astonishment or perplexity, or maybe even admiration.

In that case I'll help.

They got close to the bed and he slid one arm under Baby Girl's back and the other beneath her knees while Vicky cradled her head. He attempted to lift her but the pain in his ribs made him put the body back down. Fuckit, he said. He tried again and again doubled over, fuckit, and he didn't know why but knew he was about to cry.

Squat down, Vicky said. Then stand up slowly and I'll take her back too.

They did that, and as soon as he sensed that he held all her weight he stood as fast as he could.

Vicky placed Baby Girl's arms carefully on top of her body and then positioned her head like she was curled up against the Redeemer's chest.

Let's go, he said.

Vicky opened one door then ran and opened the next, as he followed in a juddering stumble of painful steps; Motherfucker, he said to each bruise and then to his whole body, Fuck you fuckin motherfucker; and then to her body: Don't you go and fall on me, Baby Girl, don't you fuckin even think about falling.

It was dark out now, but in addition to that there was something different in the atmosphere, the temperature had dropped and the air had finally come unstuck; it wasn't exactly windy but you could tell wind was on the cards. And the sky was clear and there was light coming from below.

You want me to help you? asked the Neeyanderthal, seeing him on the verge of collapse.

No.

Then carry her properly, this ain't luggage you're delivering.

I know that.

He saw Dolphin's truck round one corner. He and the Unruly were alone. They got out and the Neeyanderthal approached to check for gats or shanks or other instruments of slaughter.

The Redeemer straightened up tall and strode to the other corner, where the towering silhouette of the Mennonite, the fidgety shapes of the Castro kids and the tip of the father's cigarette could be discerned. Behind them a black hearse. Romeo's mother wasn't coming. Sometimes mothers come out to collect their children, other times they stay home no matter what, to make sure their children have a place prepared for them when they get back.

The Mennonite took a few steps forward then stopped and stood before the Redeemer. He looked Baby Girl over carefully.

Any need to inspect her?

None at all. I trust you're delivering Romeo exactly as he was yesterday?

Every inch untouched.

The Mennonite turned and walked back to the corner, circled the hearse and came back, boy in arms. The Neeyanderthal received him, and almost simultaneously the Redeemer delivered Baby Girl to her brothers. Up until that moment the families had been silent, but when the Neeyanderthal got close with Romeo, the Unruly stepped back and started sobbing disconsolately, shrieking with her mouth covered, hands choking back her cries. Trembling, it took her several small steps to make it to her brother tho she wasn't far at all, and then finally she embraced him and cried on his chest. On the other side, the Castro brothers were placing Baby Girl into the hearse and weeping but not allowing themselves to sob. Their father shook his head slowly side to side; then, suddenly, he took a decisive step toward Dolphin, and the Mennonite took another in case he tried anything, but all the man did was point at the hearse, glowing ember at the end of his hand, and open his mouth without finding any words, until finally he said They told me she got sick, that you didn't kill her, and I believe them, but what call was there to go and fuck us over like this? All for what? Fighting over ashes.

They were my ashes, Dolphin said. And when he said it he sounded as if he possessed a strength he no longer did, said it without wheezing, with that lung he'd been missing for years.

The other man waited a few seconds before replying. You're right. But Baby Girl's not to blame for that.

Dolphin had nothing more to say. The other man turned back to the hearse and opened the door to get in.

She never liked being called that, the Unruly shouted after him, and he turned to look. I have a name, that's what she said the day I took her home with me, don't call me Baby Girl. And she told me her name.

The Castro patriarch glanced at her a second then said I know my daughter's name.

And he got into the hearse. Before following him, the Mennonite came over to say goodbye. They bumped fists.

You going back home? The Redeemer asked.

Nah. I don't even know if there's anywhere to go back to.

The Redeemer approached the Unruly and said Give him a call.

She looked at him, uncomprehending.

Your brother-in-law.

The Unruly nodded yes and turned.

The Neeyanderthal accompanied the Fonsecas to their truck and placed Romeo into the box. Since they were going different directions, the families crossed each other once more, but this time no one looked. So many things had been hurled, things written in stone, that the street lay in ruins.

The Redeemer watched the hearse drive away. Who will bury that girl? he wondered. Because it won't be them, those who wept so much and threatened so much, they won't be the ones to dig her grave. When did we stop burying those we love with our own hands? he thought. From people like us, what the hell can we expect?

A cold breeze began, timidly. The Neeyanderthal rubbed his hands together and said What now? You got juice?

No, Neeyan, Vicky said. It's time to go. Each of us will clean our guts our own way.

Okay, the Neeyanderthal replied, and looked the Redeemer up and down. I'd say I hope your way involves getting it on with the neighbor, but shit, state you're in I think you'll keel over before you can say bless my soul.

He gave him a rough pat on the back and said We're outta here.

Vicky came to give him a kiss and, right as she was about to, turned to one side and sneezed into her elbow.

Maybe one day people wouldn't even remember when everyone had started doing it like that, instead of covering their noses with their hands. It takes a serious scare for some gestures to take hold but then they end up like scars that seem to have been there all along. Maybe they themselves would one day be nothing but someone's scar, nameless, no epitaph, just a line on the skin.

Because like everything, this too would pass, and the world would act innocent for a while, until it scared them shitless once more.

The two of them left, and the Redeemer entered the Big House. He tried to remember a good mantra but the only thing that came to mind was Let them burn me and turn me, mark me and merk me—and that wasn't what he wanted.

Three Times Blonde opened the door and the Redeemer walked in.

She took a look at his split lip and stroked the scab on his head.

People are fools, she said. They spend their whole lives getting stuck with pins and act like nothing's wrong, they just leave them there, and then one day they go and scratch someone's eyes out.

The truth is, the Redeemer said, maybe we're damned from the start.

What truth? Three Times Blonde looked at him like he was an idiot. I don't buy that crap, that *Look but don't touch* stuff. Tell me, what truth? Maybe someone out there knows, but it's not me, so I call it like I see it.

And she poked a dieresis into his chest.

The Redeemer placed a hand on her back and ran it all the way down and over the curve of her ass.

Plus, she went on, they said on TV people are getting better now, that they really know what it is and there's no reason to die.

They pressed up against the wall and the Redeemer kissed her a bit of his blood. Suddenly Three Times Blonde cocked her head and said Listen.

A wavering windstorm was blowing outside the Big House. Maybe the clouds are gone, she said, and let go of the Redeemer.

The Redeemer observed her profile, so luscious and tuned-in to the sounds on the street. Talk and cock is all I got, he thought. And sometimes fear.

I'm tired of being cooped up, Three Times Blonde said.

She walked out into the hall and then onto the street and the Redeemer followed, but before he caught up to her at the front door, la Ñora's opened.

Are your visitors gone?

They are, señora, thank you for your discretion.

Young man, said la Ñora. You knew, didn't you?

The Redeemer had known, but he also knew sometimes it was best not to say. So he said nothing.

He got mad and left, la Ñora went on. And I thought I'd never hear from him again, that's the way it is these days, people just disappear, but someone called from the courts, a young lady he told to phone me. I don't know why they're holding him. He says he's black and blue but they've stopped beating him now.

La Ñora paused to allow the Redeemer to intervene and he hoped against hope that she wasn't asking what she seemed to be asking.

I'm going to go get him, la Ñora said. Do you know where the place is?

Fuckit, she was, she was asking. For a moment he considered the possibility of letting the little sonofabitch spend the night in the hoosegow but he couldn't do it. Perhaps Gustavo was right: these days we walk past a body on the street, and we have to stop pretending we can't see it.

Aren't you afraid you might get whatever this is? he asked her.

Me? I don't get anything anymore, not even tired.

Best not to go out, señora, I'll get him and bring him back to you, I just have to do one thing first.

250

Thank you, young man.

He headed for the door.

Young man, said la Ñora.

The Redeemer turned.

I didn't ask for this.

The Redeemer nodded.

He turned. Be right back, he said to himself. And he opened the Big House door and went out to look at the stars once again.

TRANSLATOR'S NOTES

LISA DILLMAN

THE TRICK TO TRANSLATING RHYTHM, TONE, AND SLANG IN *KINGDOM CONS*

Kingdom Cons is a novel with music at its core, and there's no doubt that Yuri Herrera calls the tunes. On the surface level, the book is "about" a singer-songwriter—a corrido-writing accordion player, to be precise. The protagonist is a young man who is known, at different points in his life and career, as both Lobo and The Artist. He learns early on that school is not a place for him and that songs will save his life (despite later learning that they may also jeopardize it). Abandoned by both of his parents, Lobo takes up his accordion ("Now hold it good . . . This is your bread," says his father the day before upping sticks) and begins to compose. Much of the novel chronicles the transformation he undergoes after getting a gig at the Palace where he is employed to write and play corridos (ballads) in praise of the King's infinite valor, power and general badassery. The Artist's songs are all the rage with the general public and music to the ears of the King himself, and therein lies his limited clout.

Like all three of Yuri Herrera's novels to date, *Kingdom Cons* presents us with a central character who is tough and yet sensitive, lives in a cruel and violent world yet finds tenderness, and—most importantly—is aware of the fact that he wields a form of influence which derives from words and the power of communication. Also, although it is in *Kingdom Cons* where literal music-making takes center stage, musicality is central to each of Yuri's novels. And when it comes to translating the book, as central as the tune-filled plot is the rhythmic prose (or poetry, arguably), which is full of chords that are deceptively difficult to strike.

Herrera's tone can be lyrical, stentorian, strident or staccato but always manages to seem improvised, almost offhanded and utterly natural. Descriptions are often in a higher register, full of sonorous finery whether reflecting The Artist's early awe and naivete at the splendor surrounding the King or his later disillusionment and resolve. These descriptions seem almost to glide, their flow smooth; in musical terms, reflections of this sort might be seen as legato. Much of the dialogue, on the other hand, leans slangward and is short and clipped. *Kingdom Cons* is full of thugs, and they speak like thugs, their cadence more staccato. The novel also contains very poetic sections, frequently presented as stand-alone vignettes—short marcato chapters that express the Artist's inner-reflections or provide some insight into what made him the way he is. These sui generis verses are more philosophical or existential in nature. They are expressed in ways that make little sense at all if translated literally and as such—like poetry—depend even more heavily upon sound, rhythm and interpretation. The tenor of the prose, thus, changes frequently, and its rhythms in and of themselves constitute a kind of meaning.

To illustrate this, let me give two examples.

To start with, when Lobo arrives at the Palace for the first time, he is taken with all of the opulence therein, and his sense of wonder is reflected in a beautiful passage in which he describes the sorts of people he sees. Then he listens, struck dumb by the variety of men and women he's never before encountered.

> (S)e orilló a los corros y paró la oreja con hambre de saber. Escuchó de cordilleras, de selvas, de golfos, de montañas, en sonsonetes que nunca había oído: yes como shes, pal-abras sin eses a las claras se notaba que no *eran de tierra pareja*. [emphasis mine]

> Lobo **sidled up to circles**, he pricked up his ears, **thirst**-ing to **learn**. He heard tell of mountains, of jungles, of gulfs, of summits, in singsong accents entirely new to him: **yesses** like **shesses**, words with no **esses**: . . . it was **clear** they were from *nowhere near **here***. [emphasis mine]

In addition to the mellifluous flow of the Spanish, there are other things going on here: a conscious reflection on the musicality of language itself, an enumeration that serves as a rhythmic backbone, and a falling tone at the end which acts as a solemn proclamation and provides sonic finality. In addition, although "orillar" means "to pull over" or "to approach" (as well as multiple other things) in this context, it comes, quite beautifully, from the Spanish for "shore" (*orilla*), and thus hints at the topography in the enumeration in the following sentence.

In an attempt to carry across some of the sonic qualities of the original, I did a few things. A more literal translation of the first sentence might read "Lobo approached circles and raised his ear with hunger to learn," which would judder the flow. "Sidle" allows for some alliteration, and using "thirst" over "hunger" provides assonance with "learn." My choices express a desire to create an analogous effect, a means of expressing wonder via sonorous prose. After the percussive enumeration, the second sentence could more directly be rendered "y's like sh's, words without s's . . . clearly one noted that they were not from a similar land." Fortuitously, the "y" and "sh" in the Spanish refer to an accent (generally Argentine and Uruguayan) that actually corresponds to pronouncing "yes" like "shess," so that phrase can be rendered in English with almost no strategizing required (a feat uncommon in translation in general and rare indeed in Yuri). At the end of the sentence, I've made a few sonic decisions, creating an internal rhyme with *clear* and *here*, n-alliteration with *nowhere* and *near*, and insuring the falling tone of last words by using two monosyllables (*near*, *here*). In this case, the echo of "shore" (which readers of the Spanish might or might not consciously note, in the way English readers might or might not think of a rooster when calling someone "cocky") is lost, but I'll circle back to that that in a minute.

Two short pages later, the Jeweler notices Lobo staring at one man in particular and initiates a brief exchange. His comments are colloquial and slangy (and regional), and their cadence very different from the above description, relying on short words and pauses until the end.

—Ese es el Chaca . . . Entrón el bato, güevudo, pero alzadito, eso sí. No diga que se lo dije, colega . . . no hay que hacer chismes. Aquí la cosa es llevarse bien con todos y le va bien.

Because this is so informal there's no way to translate it literally, but a close approximation that doesn't consider register or connotation might look something like this: "That is the Expert . . . Daring, the guy, big balls, but a little raised up, yes that. Don't tell that I told you, colleague . . . one must not make gossip. Here the thing is to get along well with all and it goes well for you." As might be clear from the stiltedness of this attempt at literality, most of the nouns and adjectives prior to the last sentence are markedly informal: "chaca" is slang used in Northern Mexico to refer to leaders, people in charge. "Entrón", "güevudo" and "alzadito" in addition to being slang also each have suffixes attached to them. But despite the fact that -ón and –udo are augmentatives and –ito a diminutive, none of them need be literal. Thus saying "alzadito", for instance, doesn't actually mean "slightly alzado" and serves as more of a way to temper a comment; likewise, "güevudo" (a phonetic "misspelling" of "huevudo") means that someone is ballsy—large or not. Clearly, then, there is an awful lot being signified in very few words. In English:

That's the **Top Dog** . . . Punk's got balls. Fearless as they come, but he's **cocky** as shit . . . But don't say I said so, amigo. Way it works here is, you make nice with the **pack**, you'll do fine.

Shorter words, here, help produce a more broken staccato rhythm for this man's comments, and their terseness is logical

259

given that the Jeweler is giving Lobo, whom he's never met, insider knowledge at a banquet, surrounded by people. Top Dog is a name I like for a few reasons: the two monosyllables are emphatic, double stressed; it doesn't call him the Boss (which obviously can only be the King himself); it makes him an animal, and we'll come to learn that he's a rabid one. It also allows to bring in a reference to a gang of animals, making clear that everyone at the Palace is part of a pack, even if the Artist is only a lap dog. In order to lower the register of the Jeweler's comments, eliminating the definite article "the" ("Punk's got balls . . . " and "Way it works . . . ") marks the informality and orality, as does the man's use of "amigo." This choice also allows for readily comprehensible Spanish, which means *not* having to opt for a more "located" term such as "dude" or "mate." I don't italicize this or other Spanish words in order not to mark them as exotic or even foreign.

As for the Top Dog's description, "alzado" is generally taken to mean something like rebellious and derives from "alzar" (to raise). Cocky is a more colloquial way to refer to someone who's "raised up," i.e. high on themselves, and it obliquely teases out the animal references present. This type of decision translators refer to as compensation, i.e. the act of making up for something you weren't able to do in one instance (create a rhyme, make a joke or pun, etc.) by doing something analogous elsewhere. Sound and rhythm, tone and cadence, these are elements of Yuri's prose that are as integral as the story itself so it's vital to "translate" them as well. I don't mean to imply, though, that this particular decision was made to compensate for the indirect allusion to "shore" in "orillar." I am not nearly that mathematical and don't keep lists of which word or phrase is being used to make up for which rhyme or slang term or alliteration. If I did, I'd spend all day making spreadsheets, when what I want to be doing is translating!

—Decatur, Georgia, June 2017

ON THE DELICATE QUESTION OF TONE IN
SIGNS PRECEDING THE END OF THE WORLD

There could hardly be a more appropriate time for the English publication of Yuri Herrera's *Signs Preceding the End of the World*. For, in its nine short chapters, this remarkable novel explores not only the timeless themes of epic journey, death, and the underworld, but also many of the pressing issues of our times: migration, immigration (and two of its stomach-churning corollaries, so-called nativism and profiling), trans-nationalism, transculturalism, and language hybridity—not to mention, of course, the end of the world.

How, then, to recreate all of this in English? Undertaking a translation requires first determining what makes the text in question so striking, and, in the case of *Signs*, that turns out to be quite a long list. In the same way that the novel delves into a large number of themes within a very short space, Yuri Herrera's prose, too, exhibits a multitude of distinct characteristics, displaying great variations in what is always creative and often non-standard language: its rhythm and orality; a style that is elegantly spare; striking metaphors, which are often unusual but rarely jarring; a mix of registers both low and high—slang and colloquial but also lyrical and eloquent, some rural and others urban and both often very Mexican (or very much of its border); and neologism, to name just some. There is also the overall tone, which is intimate and often infused with understated affection and tenderness. And there is the fact that all of this manages to sound entirely natural. Yuri Herrera's use of language is nothing short of stunning, and translating it is both fulfilling and daunting; what makes his writing so unique is what makes it so challenging to translate.

To prepare for the project, as many translators do, I first read widely. I read for theme; I read for tone; I read for style. I read texts that took place on borders. I read about Aztec mythology and *Alice in Wonderland* and Dante's circles of hell. I tried to read writers who might have styles, or tones, or non-standard usage that I would find in some way comparable or analogous. The most helpful was Cormac McCarthy (in particular *The Road*, another tale—coincidentally, or not?— that can be read on different levels, one of which is "the end of the world"). I made word lists and devised ways to be non-standard in English (unusual collocations, creative compound nouns, nominalization of verbs and verbalization of nouns). I looked for ways to work in alliteration to lend the English rhythm, to lend it sonority. And even if much of this was culled during successive revisions and edits, these strategies informed the entire undertaking of the project, leaving their mark.

In addition, I tried to create an English that was geographically non-explicit, although, like me, the translation speaks mostly American English. To explain what I mean by that, let me offer a couple of examples. The novel's dialogues are often peppered with language—colloquialisms, slang, expressions, culturally-embedded references—that could only take place in Mexico (or on the Mexico–USA border). Translating only

what readers might see as the *meaning* of these conversations
and references might arguably produce a comprehensible and
accurate text, though it would lose its regional flavor and
intimacy (think of the difference between "a bonnie lass" and
"a pretty girl," for instance). Nevertheless, attempting to find
an English dialect that would serve as a linguistic "parallel" is
problematic. Should Mexican gangsters speak like mobsters
in *The Godfather*? If not, is there another group they should
speak like? My answer is "no." Instead, I've endeavored to do
two things. First, I have sometimes "marked" the language as
non-standard in ways that are not geographically recognizable. In dialogues, this meant emphasizing the oral nature of
the language (using colloquialisms such as "yond" for "over
there," abbreviating "about" to "bout," for example). Second, I
have occasionally left specific words in Spanish, deliberately
choosing not to translate. When a character calls his mother
jefecita, for example (literally, "little boss"—a not terribly
uncommon term of endearment), she remains *jefecita* in the
translation. My intention here is to leave a linguistic reminder
to the reader that this is, in fact, a translated text, and to avoid
renderings ("momma," "moms," etc.) that might be genuinely
intimate, but cringe-makingly American for language meant
to come out of a rural Mexican teenager's mouth.

Unsurprisingly, I also spent a tremendous amount of
time considering possibilities for the novel's most talked-
about neologism: *jarchar*. Yuri himself has discussed this
verb in multiple places. Within *Signs*, it means, essentially,
"to leave." The word is derived from *jarchas* (from the Arabic
kharja, meaning exit), which were short Mozarabic verses or
couplets tacked on to the end of longer Arabic or Hebrew

poems written in Al-Andalus, the region we now call Spain. Written in the vernacular, these lyric compositions served as a sort of bridge between cultures and languages, Mozarabic being a kind of hybrid that was, of course, not yet Spanish. And on one level *Signs* is just that: a book about bridging cultures and languages. *Jarchar*, too, is a noun-turned-verb. I wrangled with myself—and spoke somewhat obsessively with others—over how best to render this term, debating multiple options before finally deciding on "to verse" (the two runners-up were "to port" and "to twain"). Used in context it is easily understood, and has the added benefits of also being a noun-turned-verb, a term clearly referring to poetry, and part of several verbs involving motion and communication (traverse, reverse, converse) as well as the "end" of the universe. Makina, the protagonist, is the character who most often "verses," as well as the woman who serves as a bridge between cultures, languages and worlds. Would readers realize any of this had it not just been explained? I doubt it. But that's ok; the same is true of the Spanish. Opening with a sinkhole large enough to kill people and closing with another subterranean sequence, the book takes us full circle in a variety of ways.

This translation has benefited from the direct and indirect input of many people whom I'd like to thank. It was Katherine Silver who initially sent the opportunity to translate Yuri my way. I also gained from the encouragement, suggestions, edits, discussions, pep talks, emails, readings, and other forms of support of friends, mentors, and editors including Peter Bush, Jean Dangler, Lorna Scott Fox, Daniel Hahn, Henry Reese, Samantha Schnee, and Lawrence Venuti. I would like especially to thank Drew Whitelegg for multiple re-readings, endless discussions and encouragement. And my absolute deepest thanks go to Yuri himself, for answering hundreds of emails (often many per day, sometimes with a dozen questions each) as well as generously discussing in person some of the novel's many nuances, providing constant encouragement and always being open to exploring new avenues of interpretation.

—*Decatur, Georgia, February 2014*

ON THE GENIUS OF YURI HERRERA'S CHARACTER
NAMES IN *THE TRANSMIGRATION OF BODIES*

As a devout lexophile and voracious reader, I very much like the phrase *What's your read on this?* It seems a particularly apt expression when applied to Yuri Herrera's texts. There are many possible reads on books like *Signs Preceding the End of the World* or *The Transmigration of Bodies*, perhaps as many reads as there are readers, yet somehow they seem to concur on one thing: that Yuri Herrera can pack a huge amount into a short novel. As his translator, I've often seen him pack just as much into a single word, and every time he makes it seem effortless, natural, almost off-the-cuff. As a tribute to this, therefore, I wanted to shed a little light on an aspect of the book that may not be available to most readers of the English edition: the characters' names. Yuri's prose has a strikingly beautiful density to it; he does so many things at once, plays on so many levels simultaneously: genre, register, history, reference and allusion, etc. Perhaps unsurprisingly, this made some characters' names very challenging to translate.

The density of Yuri's prose, its multifaceted compactness, is also why *The Transmigration of Bodies*, like *Signs Preceding the End of the World*, is difficult to adequately sum up. You might say that it's a tale of two feuding families with Shakespearean undertones, or that it's the story of the protagonist's tortured soul, or of a man struggling to come to terms with his life and the way he fits in—or doesn't—to the society around him. And of course there's a rich and multi-layered commentary that emerges from background, in which a mysterious mosquito-borne epidemic has gridlocked an unspecified and militarized Mexican city. But a glib overview of what the book is *about* doesn't paint a very satisfactory or nuanced picture of what the novel *does*. To me, in many ways what it does is present a series of reflections. It's a reflection on death (and the ways that death gets used). It's a reflection on violence (and the ways that violence gets used). It's a reflection on human contact, both carnal and fraternal-slash-sororal (and the ways that human contact gets used). It's a reflection on language (and the ways that language gets used). That's an awful lot of food for thought, and in my view one of the pleasures of the text is that, rather than denounce this and advocate that, *Transmigration* induces us to contemplate, to mull things over, to ponder. And perhaps to try to be more tender, to show a bit more empathy. And Yuri's names are there to help us do this.

To shed a little light on what I mean, I'll talk about the names of two characters, and their translations. The most obvious name is that of the Redeemer, the hardboiled protagonist we meet mid-hangover on page one (although his name does not in fact appear until page 26). In Spanish he's called "el Alfaqueque," which is a word you won't find in Spanish-English dictionaries (nor is it in that many Spanish-Spanish dictionaries). But those who have studied Spanish might remember that all words beginning *al-* originally come from the Arabic. "Alfaqueque" derives from *fakka al-aseer*, meaning to emancipate, ransom or redeem. In the Middle Ages, alfaqueques in the Iberian Peninsula were those appointed to negotiate the release of Christians being held captive by Moors. They are described in the *Siete Partidas*, which was essentially a code of laws compiled in the thirteenth century: alfaqueques were considered men of honor who used their knowledge of Arabic to interpret and negotiate the captives' release.

So that's our protagonist's name in (medieval) Spanish. Now for the English. Clearly, as far as holding on to the Arabic etymology goes, there's no viable English option. So what should the guy be called in translation? I toyed with several possibilities. Given the novel's often hardboiled tone, I considered names like the Fixer, the Interpreter, the Messenger and the Negotiator. Each had its appeal. The Fixer I felt had more of a mafia ring to it; the Interpreter put more stress on his linguistic aptitude, which the novel makes clear is absolutely vital (and the word is four syllables, like the original, which I liked a lot). The Messenger might have a little more Shakespearean resonance, which is also important, while the Negotiator, in addition to connoting his role as a go-between, struck me as more involved, more active. Yet at the same time, to my ear, all of them had a modern almost Hollywood sound that I felt cheapened them somehow. I could almost hear the Morgan Freeman voiceover. So despite honestly liking all of those options, in the end I decided they were too contemporary-sounding.

If you look at historical documents and speak to medievalists, alfaqueques are often referred to as both ransomers and redeemers (indeed, these are the terms used when people speak about the *Partidas* in English). Redeemer was the option I chose for several reasons. Historical accuracy is important, certainly, so the fact that English translations

of the *Partidas* use the term played a large role. But there
is more to it than that. The word alfaqueque is incredibly
sonorous. I don't know how to do phonetic transcription,
but in Spanish it's pronounced *ahl-fah-KEH-keh*. It rolls off
the tongue, it should be in poems, it should be your favorite
word. Redeemer is not as beautiful, but it is more stentorian,
and also more resonant and polysemous than the previous
options. And that mattered to me. What I'm trying to say is,
the word *redeemer* opens up a range of meanings and connotations, expanding or deepening possible interpretations of
the character's role. For instance, you have, of course, the
religious connotations of redemption, which are interesting
to poke at, given the often "unchristian" behavior of the
protagonist. And I would call that tension complicated and
fruitful, rather than ironic or hypocritical, because religious
redemption is very tied up with concepts of death and souls
and of right and wrong; and what more fitting for the milieu
of this novel? The possibility of a certain savior-like allusion
when you're referring to a man who makes his living as a
fixer is pretty nifty, in my book. In addition to that is the
more commercial sense of redeeming, i.e. the exchanging or
regaining of things. And this type of redemption is quite
literally what the protagonist spends much of the novel
doing, wrangling a way to redeem the bodies (while searching
his soul and trying to get laid). So in the end, it's fair to say
that the Redeemer might be the most literal translation of
his name, but that's not why I chose it. As I said, Yuri plays
with genre, register, history, reference and allusion. And I
think Redeemer is the name that best gets at that: historical
accuracy, old language, and multiple possible nuances and

connotations. Plus it still potentially sounds like the guy could be a badass.

In utter contrast to the Redeemer is the protagonist's romantic rival, the boyfriend of Three Times Blonde. While the Redeemer's name is foreign, venerable and archaic, the boyfriend's is the complete opposite: cheesy, modern and utterly lacking in nuance and subtlety. So right away you have an interplay of registers. As characters, too, they couldn't be more different. Whereas the Redeemer is portrayed as un-studly, poorly dressed, insecure (despite a certain degree of luck with the ladies) and actually quite sensitive (think of his respect for the dead, the tenderness he shows la Ñora, the degree of thought he puts into touch), the boyfriend is cocksure, garish, superficial and no doubt an idiot. After all, the man named his car Bronco. And his monikers reflect this. Although he's generally referred to in more or less the same way, he doesn't have a single-word name and he's not always capitalized. But generally, the boyfriend is referred to as something like the "slicked-back baby jack." It's hard, if not impossible, to exaggerate how much thought, time, research and effort went in to coming up with this. Debates with myself and others were endless, and I literally had pages and pages of terms, words and partial options. I would wake up in the night with an idea (I started keeping a pad and pencil by my bed), only to realize the next morning that on one level or another it didn't work. Thankfully, Tara Tobler, editor par excellence, was happy to discuss, and discuss, and discuss the pros and cons of many of those.

The original Spanish is "hamponcito relamido patrás." Like the word alfaqueque, the boyfriend's nickname actually amazingly sonorous, albeit in a derisory rather than majestic way. It's also something that conjures up an image instantly. And yet linguistically it's incredibly complicated. The word *hampón* is a fairly uncommon word that means "thug," and *–cito* is a diminutive stuck on the end, so already the man is being taken down a few pegs, has a sort of pathetic wannabe flavor to him. The second word, *relamido*, can mean many different things. On its own, according to *Collins* it means: "affected," "prim and proper," "overdressed," "cheeky" and "shameless." But the verb it comes from (*lamer/re-lamer*) means "to lick" (repeatedly). And then when you add *patrás* it gains new meaning, making it refer—at least potentially—to hair, i.e. hair that has been greased back. Think Brylcreem. Finally, *patrás* is a combination of two words, *para* and *atrás*, i.e. "toward the back," but written as it would be pronounced, something along the lines of *gonna* in English. So it's quite a mouthful. The boyfriend is, of course, a pretty oily character, so having "slick" in his name seemed appropriate, although for a long time my options revolved around "grease" and "greased." But overall, the hardest thing to do was attempt to capture the ring of the entire nickname, the way all of it sounds when strung together. The cadence, the number of syllables, where the stress lies when you say it out loud, all of these things are crucial to the rhythm of the text. In the end, I really love the name he's got and hope readers will too. And I couldn't be more thrilled and thankful that Three Times Blonde is a word-for-word literal translation that required no deliberation whatsoever. (A rarity in literary translation, a miracle in a text by the breathtakingly talented Yuri Herrera.)

—*Decatur, Georgia, June 2016*